CHILD OF PASSION

Penelope was the child of Lettice and
Walter Devereux, but neither parent gave
her love or security. She was married
to Lord Rich when Philip Sidney fell
passionately in love with her and poured
out his feelings in his poetry. After
Sidney's death, Penelope's life became
more complex, as she had seven children
by Rich and five by her lover, Charles
Blount. She managed to keep the two
families separate, the two men satisfied
and the Elizabethan court in ignorance.
The acknowledged beauty of her time,
Penelope's fascination lasted to the end
of her colourful life.

CHILD OF PASSION

CHILD
OF PASSION

by
Judith Saxton

Dales Large Print Books
Long Preston, North Yorkshire,
England.

British Library Cataloguing in Publication Data.

Saxton, Judith
    Child of passion.

    A catalogue record for this book is
    available from the British Library

    ISBN 1-85389-885-6 pbk

First published in Great Britain by Robert Hale Ltd., 1978

Copyright © 1978 by Judy Turner

Cover illustration © Melvyn Warren-Smith by arrangement
with P.W.A. International Ltd.

The moral right of the author has been asserted

Published in Large Print 1999 by arrangement with Judy
Turner & The Caroline Shelden Literary Agency.

Dales Large Print is an imprint of
Library Magna Books Ltd.
Printed and bound in Great Britain by
T.J. International Ltd., Cornwall, PL28 8RW.

The story of one dizzy
blonde for another.
My dear friend, Thelma Walshaw

Stella, sovereign of my joy,
Fair triumpher of annoy,
Stella, star of heavenly fires,
Stella, lode-star of desires;

Stella, in whose body is
Writ each character of bliss,
Whose face all, all beauty passeth,
Save thy mind, which yet surpasseth!

Philip Sidney

ONE

Toothache had sent her uneasily from her bed, ranging the house like a restless little ghost, unable to find comfort. She padded across the room she shared with her sister Dorothy, seeing the moonlight dappling the walls with an indifferent eye. She prowled restlessly up the corridor, so preoccupied with the raging pain in her mouth that she scarcely felt the cold, and entered the nursery where her young brothers slept.

Robert, her father's heir, lay in the little fourposter with the faded blue curtains, where she had once slept. Even in her pain, the child smiled lovingly at her favourite brother, his face rosy and innocent in sleep, his lashes making dark circles on his cheeks. Beside him lay nurse, looking even more fat and comfortable without her stiff cap and boned bodice, drowned in slumber.

Once, she remembered wistfully, nurse's attention and love had been hers by right. But now she was grown-up, all of seven years old, and it was no use crying when her teeth hurt her as they cut through the tender gums.

'You must endure it, Penelope,' her mother had said impatiently, her lovely face cold, her light voice colder.

It was Lady Devereux's impatience and her barely concealed distaste for her daughter which made Penelope shrink from waking anyone. For her mother worshipped beauty and despised ugliness, and since she knew she was not beautiful, she should not expect sympathy for her pain.

Normally, she told herself, it did not matter if no-one cuddled her, for she was the eldest; a big girl. But now her heart yearned for the gentle voice, the loving touch, which she had once known. Oh, to be a baby again, safe in the nursery, with love and concern awake and within reach if you whimpered!

At this point in her wandering she reached the head of the stairs and glanced hopefully down into the hall below. But no light showed, except for the squares of moonlight which flooded through the tall window facing her.

Penelope began to descend; after all, she could not sleep, and would not disturb anyone by walking the deserted house.

Reaching the hall, she hesitated; which way to go? Then she thought of her mother's sitting room, and her pace quickened. The fire would not have been out long, for her mother was never early to bed. She could curl up in the big velvet chair with its deep, feather cushions, and hold out her toes to the embers. Brightening, she remembered that the last time she had cut a tooth she had forgotten her new-found maturity and appealed to nurse. And Goody had warmed a piece of flannel and bidden her hold it over the sore gum. Then she had brewed a soothing posset, and when it was drunk down to the last drop Penelope had curled up on nurse's fat lap and fallen asleep at once.

Heartened by this recollection, she opened the door of the sitting room and slipped inside. The fire *did* still glow! She crossed the room quietly, not needing the patches of moonlight to guide her, and sat down in the big chair. A cushion, held out to the embers, soon warmed, and she laid her cheek on its comforting softness. Her feet began to tingle pleasantly, and an enormous sense of well-being enveloped her. Soon, she was sure, the pain would begin to ebb, it seemed less intense already with the arms of the chair curving round her almost like a mother's arms.

Above her, a shawl hung over the back of her retreat and she pulled it down and cuddled it round her, enjoying the extra warmth and the traces of her mother's sharp, sweet perfume which still clung to the folds. She smiled sleepily, as snug as a kitten, and as content. Her lids, heavy from the unaccustomed night-prowling, began to droop.

She was on the very borders of sleep when a sudden sound brought her eyes wide in the darkness, making her heart beat like a drum. She peeped cautiously round the wing of her chair as the door swung slowly open. Heart in mouth, she suddenly remembered something she had heard her mother discussing with an aunt, once. Devereux women, she had said, have a foreknowledge of their own deaths, for just before the last illness, they meet a shade of themselves so perfect that even the last detail of the dress is the same, like seeing oneself in a mirror.

Could toothache prove fatal? Would she presently see entering the room a thin little seven-year-old, in a long white shift, with a shawl bunched around her shoulders?

At first, all she saw was a tall candle,

dripping wax onto the polished floor, but it was too high to be held by any child, whether ghost or quick.

Mother will be cross, Penelope thought, as sweet relief flooded through her, and almost in the same breath realised it *was* her mother. But so different from the cool, impatient woman who had brushed her daughter aside earlier in the evening! For Lady Devereux was ... rumpled, thought Penelope incredulously. Her beautiful green silk gown had slipped off one shoulder, and her beautiful red-gold hair was loose, flowing freely across her milky breast.

She was not alone. A man had called to see Walter Devereux that day, walking coolly into Chartley with the arrogance shared by most courtiers of Elizabeth I, and said in a fashionable drawl that he would await the master's return.

He had not seemed particularly friendly with her mother, yet here he was with his arm round her waist, his free hand moving shamelessly across her body!

Even as Penelope watched, the man pulled her mother close and their lips met in a long kiss. Shocked, Penelope heard her mother laugh on a low, intimate note as they drew apart, saying, 'What a way to treat your hostess, Robert!'

The man laughed too, his teeth gleamingly wolfishly in his dark beard.

'You are so much warmer than Queen Elizabeth, Letty,' he murmured. 'More generous as well.'

'The Queen would kill us both if she knew,' Lady Devereux said on a half-laughing, half-serious note. 'And I am a married woman.'

'I have no ties of that nature, Letty.'

'You may not be married, Robert, but you are tied to her grace, for all that.'

'In the spirit perhaps, but not the body. And the body has its appetites, even though they're dangerous.'

He moved as he spoke, seeming to Penelope to be manoeuvring her mother over to where a thick white sheepskin rug lay at the foot of another velvet-covered chair.

Lady Devereux said, 'Quietly, my love,' in a throaty whisper, and then Penelope heard the chair creak as it received their weight.

They were out of her range of vision now, and she curled yet lower in the chair, pulling the shawl over her head, willing herself to sleep so that the murmurs and movements would not tempt her to peep.

But she was no longer shocked; not even when she heard a rustle and a soft hissing sound, and saw her mother's green silk gown go sliding along the floor, carrying with it the elegant gentleman's dark crimson hose. Her mother's behaviour she knew to be unconventional, to say the least. But could it be wrong to love, if love took the coldness from Lady Devereux, and from the great Sir Robert Dudley? Because of their caresses their voices were softened, their laughter muted and gentle.

When I am grown I will love like that, Penelope vowed. I will lie on a sheepskin rug and make throaty murmurs and sigh, and then I will laugh a little, but kindly; and the next day I will be cold and proud again, and no-one need know that I can be cuddly and warm as well, save for my lover.

She did not hear them leave but she must have slept, for the next thing she knew was the sun hot on her face and she could hear the faint sound of servants stirring. She knelt up and looked over the back of her chair. The room was deserted. She looked in vain for a sign of last night's rendezvous—then saw the sheepskin rug was askew on the polished oak. So she had not dreamed it, it had really happened!

Yawning, she struggled to her feet, automatically putting her finger to her mouth. No pain now, but the sharp point of the new tooth. Greatly relieved, she jumped across to the warmth of the rug, and from there padded across the floor. She would slip into bed beside Dorothy and no-one need ever know that she had strayed.

It was the work of a moment to run up the stairs and along the corridor to her room. Cautiously, she slipped into the bed she shared with Dorothy and wrapped her cold toes in her shift, snuggling luxuriously against her sister's warm, plump back. In the morning, she thought drowsily, I must see how mother and Sir Robert greet each other. In the morning ...

TWO

'But sir,' Philip had said furiously, 'She's only a little *girl!*' That had been when the match was first mooted by his adoring parent.

Now, he stood in the big hall at Chartley

where he had stood so many times before, listening to his father and Sir Walter Devereux talking. But though his attention seemed to be wholly held by the men, he eyed Penelope from time to time, whenever she seemed unconscious of his regard.

From the superior height of his twenty-two years she seemed a little girl indeed— and such a plain little girl at that! Her thin face, with the light hair strained back from her high forehead and her great black eyes staring at everything, was too intense for him; he preferred little girls to be tomboys rather than self-consciously correct, as Penelope Devereux was.

Through the window he could see the other girl, Dorothy, only a year younger after all, screaming as she chased two small boys across the lawn. The three of them made a pretty picture, and he watched them with relief for a moment, glad to escape from the idea of marriage to this pale, frightened-eyed child.

Presently, Sir Henry suggested that his

son might like to speak to the young lady and Philip, ever the gentleman, strolled over to her chair and stood beside it, smiling down at her. He noted with compassion the pink which stained her cheeks at his attention and with less pleasant feelings the adolescent spots which laced her chin and brow. However, she got to her feet with tolerable composure and dropped him a shaky curtsy.

So close to her, he could see plainly not only the spots which marred her skin but the tiny budding of her newly forming breasts, and the straightness of her thin, practical limbs.

Sighing to himself, he said, 'You have a beautiful home here, Penelope. I do not say it is magnificent because it is not, but I dare say it is pleasanter to live in than some more imposing residences.'

Penelope smiled stiffly and Philip thought uneasily that his remark had sounded condescending; he had not meant it so.

Now he said hastily, to make amends,

'Your father keeps fine horses, too. Do you have a favourite mount?'

It seemed that this was a felicitous remark because for a moment animation brightened the child's eyes, making her seem less timid.

'Yes I do,' she said. 'There is a bay mare, Swallow-foot, which I often ride. But there is another, a stallion with a coat like watered silk, black as coal—oh, he's magnificent! No-one has ridden him yet, but my father says he is too mettlesome for a woman. He thinks my brother Robert will be able to handle him though, one day.'

'And you think Robert too young for such a creature,' Philip said with understanding. 'So do I. He cannot be more than ten, I am sure.'

'He is nine, though very tall and strong for his age,' Penelope said. 'And he is the heir, of course.'

'I daresay he will let you ride the horse, when it is his own,' Philip suggested.

She nodded vigorously. 'Oh, yes. Rob is very generous, and we are good friends. When we play up at the castle ruins, or when he helps the men to cut out a bull from the herd of cattle, he lets me be his second-in-command. At least,' she amended hastily, 'He did so when I was younger, of course.'

Philip thought of the Chartley cattle, descendants, it was said, of the Aurochs, the wild cattle first domesticated by the Romans. They were mighty beasts, white save for black ears, with great branching horns and notoriously short tempers.

'You help to cut Auroch bulls out of the herd?' he said incredulously.

She blushed, and he sensed her immediate withdrawal.

'We are not allowed,' she mumbled. 'Mother would be furious if she knew I had said such an unladylike thing, and besides, it is forbidden. You won't tell her?'

He shook his head, turning slightly to watch Lettice Devereux. He had never liked Walter's wife but had to admit her undoubted attractions. Her slanting sherry gold eyes were beautiful, as was her mouth with its wayward, tilting smile, and her figure was that of a girl still, though she had borne her husband five children. But he found his Uncle Leicester's ponderous flirting with her a trifle embarrassing. Damn it, the woman was in her thirties, and respectably married and the Earl had contracted some sort of alliance with Lady Douglass Sheffield, who had borne him a son.

Philip was worldly enough to realise that poor Douglass had been but a fleeting fancy, and he had heard the rumours of the clandestine love affair between Leicester and Lettice which had been sharply quashed by the Queen. But one glance now at his uncle and Penelope's mother had proved that even if the Queen had forgotten the business, Leicester had not. The Earl's narrow, dark eyes dwelt on Lettice's vivacious little face with the air of a man who eyes a treat he has enjoyed in the past, and intends to enjoy again.

He had forgotten Penelope and was abruptly reminded of her again as she said softly, 'She *is* beautiful, isn't she? Dotty and I want to be like her when we are full-grown, but it is up-hill work. Sometimes we get very discouraged.'

'Yes, she is lovely,' Philip agreed. 'But you are young yet; too young to worry about such things.'

She nodded, accepting the remark as a rebuke and presently he bowed and moved away from her again, bored.

Did they really expect him to marry a child not yet thirteen, with no beauty, no money, and absolutely no conversation? The thought crossed his mind that perhaps she suffered from the constant comparison with Lettice, but he dismissed it; other girls had beautiful mothers but they did not allow themselves to be overshadowed to that extent. Nearer to the truth perhaps, was that she was young even for her little age. And in the meantime he had only to tell his father that he would not consider marriage with Penelope, to have that gentleman dismiss the matter from his mind. After all, she came from a family of only moderate important. To be sure, he was very fond of the Earl of Essex, but Sir Walter would understand that he could not dream of marrying when he had the whole of Europe yet to explore. Indeed, it would be hard enough to carve a name for himself, without the additional burden of a child-bride.

He greeted his father's anxious look with a speaking glance, and knew that explanations would not be necessary; it would be enough that Penelope was not the wife for him.

★ ★ ★ ★

Lettice sat before her mirror, brushing out her gleaming, coppery hair. Behind her, her plain daughter lurked, looking thinner and less attractive than ever in a red silken bed-gown and curly-toed oriental slippers.

'I'm afraid, mother, that Philip does not care for me.'

Their eyes met in the mirror, Penelope's apologetic, Lettice's amused.

'No, Pen, I'm afraid he does not,' Lettice said equably. 'But he is a very stupid young man. He thinks it clever to say what he thinks instead of wrapping the unpalatable truth in clean linen. However, it would have been a good match.'

'I'm sorry,' Penelope muttered. The colour flooded up into her cheeks and Lettice thought dispassionately that the huge dark eyes set in that thin pink face made her daughter look remarkably like a boiled prawn.

'Don't be sorry,' she said lightly. 'There are other men. He is handsome, is he not?'

Lettice thought of his strong young jaw, the lips which spoke of determination even though his blue eyes were so dreamy.

Penelope's face turned a deeper pink and she smiled at her again through the mirror, saying 'There is no need to blush! They are a good-looking family, but beauty is only skin deep; if you cannot be lovely to look at, you must be charming. I did not think you charming at dinner, Penelope. You should speak out boldly when spoken to, or remain silent. Twice I saw Philip speak to you, and you just blushed and mumbled into your food. You will never get a lover *that* way!'

'I'll try to do better. I'm sorry,' the child said, hanging her head.

The very humbleness of her tone annoyed Lettice, but she did not want to lose her temper with Penelope tonight. She drew in her breath, however, and tapped her fingers on the dressing-table top.

'Don't keep apologising,' she said sharply. 'It is not an endearing habit to be constantly sorry for what you've done. You would do better to mind your ways. Now be off with you. Tomorrow the Earl of Leicester rejoins the court at Kenilworth and I shall go with him. You will stay here. There is no reason, now, for you to accompany the court. Whilst I am gone, *do* try to learn some endearing ways! Take Robert as an example; I am sure he is lively and affectionate enough for half-a-dozen. Goodnight, daughter.'

She made the remark half mockingly, but there was nothing mocking in Penelope's deep curtsy, nor in the way the child scuttled out of the door.

Lettice sighed, and waited until the soft pad of the child's slippered feet had faded into silence, then she crossed the room and stood by the open door. A draught caught the flames of the tall wax candles on the joint stool, and they bowed and dipped lazily, as though welcoming a visitor. And as though on cue, the Earl of Leicester, shoes in hand, came up the corridor and slipped into the room, closing the door softly after him.

'Lord, you came quietly, Robert,' Lettice

said. 'I've only just dismissed Penny. A good thing you were no earlier.'

'Yes, I passed the maid, scuttling along with her head down. She was crying, and didn't notice me. What had you said to her, Letty? Given her a scolding because my nephew don't fancy her? Bless me, but I cannot understand how you came to mother such a plain child! The boys are a handsome pair, and little Dot is bright enough. But the older girl has neither looks nor charm.'

He smiled and began to undress, throwing off his clothes with the abandon of a tired man who feels himself at home.

Lettice moved across to the bed and turned down the sheet. 'Yes, she is plain,' she acknowledged. 'But your nephew thinks too much of himself. He cannot expect a child of twelve to have attained her full looks.'

'Philip is a poet, and wants beauty all around him,' Leicester said. He walked over to the bed, arrogantly naked, and caught hold of a thick swathe of Lettice's hair. 'He should study *you*, my beauty, if he wants to be driven to write poetry. God, you drive me to lengths which no woman has ever done, nor will. I risk everything for you.'

His voice thickened on the last words, and he pulled impatiently at the shift which still covered her. 'It is a warm night,' he said.

Lettice threw off the shift and for a moment they stood breast to breast, almost touching in the golden candlelight. Then she walked over to the candles and snuffed the flames with a wetted thumb and forefinger.

In the pale starlight her body showed milk-white, her hair seemed black. She walked back to Leicester again, then stood on tiptoe and pulled his head down to hers. 'We have only one night before we must meet once again as two strangers in other people's houses,' she said. 'Must we waste these brief hours with talk of Philip and Penelope?'

For answer, he lifted her in his arms and laid her on the bed.

'I need you,' he said huskily. 'One night at Kenilworth, one night here; even that is better than nothing.'

He climbed onto the bed beside her, and they spoke no more.

THREE

The coach which bore Penelope and her guardian's wife through the English countryside was entering London at last. Entranced, Penelope leaned forward in her seat and stared with all her eyes. It had been a long absence. She had been at Chartley when her father had died in Ireland, but had been brought at once to London. Once there, she, Dorothy and little Walter had met the Earl of Huntingdon and his wife, who were to take care of them until they came of age or were married.

Seeing the familiar streets now brought back the pain of that earlier loss. Not that Sir Walter had been a particularly affectionate father, but he had been deeply interested in his children, and ambitious for them. Not like mother, Penelope thought wryly.

And since the Earl's death, they had scarcely seen Lettice. Since he was the heir, Robert had been brought up by Lord Burghley, so even the children of the family had been separated. And I so love Robert, Penelope thought, remembering the nights she had lain awake and crying in her bed because the bright, intelligent little brother whom she loved had been taken away from her, and she did not know when she would see him again.

But life with Lord and Lady Huntingdon had had a pattern, a sort of continuity, which had done them all good. Dorothy, inclined to wildness, had become more calm, and Penelope knew that she herself had gained a self-assurance she had hitherto lacked. And their York home had become dear to the young Devereux. They would never forget the grey stones of the city, nor the high skies above the moors where swallows wheeled over heather purpled by summer, rusted by winter.

She had known, of course, that this peaceful existence could not last; nor, in her heart, did she want it to. She was a woman now, of marriageable age, and her mother had remarried, her new husband being the Earl of Leicester. So though the Huntingdons had arranged a marriage for her, it would be to her mother's roof that she would go until the wedding day.

She wondered about the husband who had been selected for her. Robert Rich! She had been assured that it would be an excellent match, for he was as rich as his name implied, and young. Penelope, leaning back in her seat, indulged in a little daydream. She would enter Leicester House and there, talking to her stepfather, she would see Philip Sidney, that superior young man who had not thought her pretty enough to be his wife. He would turn, and see her. Stunned by her beauty, he would advance slowly towards her, his mouth open, his eyes fixed on her face. And just as he begged to be introduced, another figure would step forward. Taller than Philip, with a more commanding presence; an altogether worthier figure. 'Ah, Sidney,' he would say in a deep, rich voice, 'Meet my future wife.' And Philip would realise that the woman he had scorned was now an acknowledged beauty, and beyond his reach. She sighed with pleasure, wriggling deeper in her corner of the coach.

'Here is Leicester House,' kind Lady Huntingdon said. 'Shake out your skirts and straighten your cloak. You must look your best for Lady Leicester.'

Penelope, nervously smiling, obediently

tidied herself. She remembered better than anything else about her mother how she always sought and expected perfection. Even when money had been lamentably short and old gowns had been turned and turned again she had always seemed elegant and well groomed.

But Kate Hastings had done her best by her charge, and most of the money which she had been paid for Penelope's upkeep this current year had gone into garments for this London visit. So Penelope knew herself to be well-dressed from her russet silk gown with honey-coloured sleeves down to her silk stockings.

Stepping gracefully down from the coach, she glimpsed her neat ankles and felt a thrill of pride in her silk clad legs, and the softness of the leather of her little mole-coloured slippers.

She glanced around her. The forecourt was spacious and paved with light coloured slabs of stone. The front door of the house was gained by a short flight of steps, and the windows stared inquisitively down at her, as though they wondered at her impertinence in standing before them.

Penelope straightened her shoulders and waved to the departing coach. Then she began, with trepidation, to mount the steps.

★ ★ ★ ★

Robert, Earl of Leicester ran lightly down the stairs and walked across the great hall towards his open front door. For a man nearing his fifties he moved with athletic ease, his breathing scarcely quickened though he had been playing with his son and heir in the nursery when his wife had called to him that her eldest daughter had arrived.

He remembered the girl, of course. A thin, diffident lass with a narrow face, the eyes too big for the breadth of it so that she looked perpetually frightened. A rabbit of a girl, or a hare.

But he had not seen her for some years and the young woman standing in the hall and looking about her was so different from his recollections that he gasped. She was tall for a woman, taller than Lady Leicester, and held herself so well that his first impression was of shapeliness and grace, topped by such abundant, golden hair that he blinked.

She finished her inspection of the hall and turned towards him. A smile tilted her lips and he was reminded of Lettice, then she said in a voice with a delightful hint of a youthful stammer, 'Lord Leicester? Do you remember me? I'm Penelope.'

He said deliberately, 'No, by God, I do *not* remember you,' and saw her flush, then smile again as she caught the intended compliment. He was enchanted, and noticed with incredulity that this primrose haired, white skinned creature had got sparkling black eyes instead of the blue he had expected.

'Your mother is upstairs, dressing to

dine with friends,' he said now, realising that his stare would soon appear rude. 'She told me to take you up to her, but you may go to your own room first, if you wish.' He had not thought to see that the room was fittingly decorated, for he had remembered her as being still a child. Now he wondered whether Letty realised what a little beauty the girl was? Who had they planned to mate her with? Ah yes, Robert Rich's boy. He had not seen the young man, who did not come often to court. Of course, Rich had been one of the wealthiest men in the kingdom and now his son had taken the title, and the money with it. But with *her* looks ... He realised he was staring again, that he'd missed her reply, and said quickly, 'I'm sorry, my dear. What was that you said?'

'I'll go straight to mother,' Penelope said. She smiled at him and he stood back so that she could mount the stairs ahead of him, and as he followed her up the flight he noticed the beautiful shape of her sloping shoulders, the narrowness of her tiny waist, and the youthful spring in her step.

By God's wounds, there can be no doubt how young Rich will feel, when he sees her, he thought. He will be mad for her.

★ ★ ★ ★

'Yes, Leicester House is very grand,' Penelope agreed politely. She stood, as she had stood so often in her childhood, behind her mother's shoulder, talking to her through the mirror whilst Lettice added the final touches to her hair and face.

'You will have a beautiful home too, when you are Lady Rich,' Lettice said. 'You have improved, Penelope. You are quite a beauty; did you know?'

Penelope felt her cheeks grow hot and knew that the hateful blush was giving her away again. Would she never be able to control her feelings, so that the blood did not rush to her face whenever she was embarrassed? But she said equably enough, 'I believe I have improved. But I am not so fair as Dotty. She has blue eyes, and the yellowest hair.'

'You will do very well,' Lettice said. 'But your stepfather and myself are dining with friends tonight. I had not thought that you would be home in time to accompany us. Did Kate Hastings have any plans for you this evening?'

'She said to have an early night, for she will call for me betimes tomorrow. I am to go to Whitehall to meet Lord Rich,' Penelope said. She looked hopefully at her mother. 'I am to wear a cream-coloured gown, embroidered with white roses in case the Queen should speak to me and be clad in colours which might clash with mine. Is he handsome, mother? Lord Rich, I mean.'

'I've never met him. But he is very rich! My, how you will impress him in cream silk, dear. Now go along to your room—it is just along the corridor—and change out of your travelling clothes. You had better dine in your room tonight, and then your woman can prepare your clothes for tomorrow. You have brought a woman?'

'Yes, I've brought Lavender Ellis—do you remember her? She is only a little older than me, and very clever at doing my hair. Mother?'

'Yes, Penelope?' Lettice said with restrained impatience.

'What do you really think of a cream gown?'

'Well, it would not have been my choice,' Lettice said dryly. 'But no doubt Kate knows best. I must drive you out now, child, or I shall be late for my engagement.'

Penelope went to her room and sat on the frail little painted chair, whilst Lavender trotted to and fro, unpacking the boxes. After only a few minutes in her mother's company her new-found self-confidence was seeping away, leaving her feeling anxious and inadequate. The cream silk was a mistake, but Lettice was too tactful to say so outright. She would look insipid and insignificant in the gown which she had loved so much until a few minutes ago. Lettice herself was wearing a green so dark that it was almost black; it showed off her coppery hair and white skin to perfection.

She toyed with the idea of changing her mind and putting on another gown next morning, but what would Lady Huntingdon say? She would probably send me back upstairs again to change, Penelope thought miserably. Very well then, she would have to wear the cream, for she knew she could never hurt Kate Hastings' feelings by criticising her choice of dress.

So if he hates me, it will be my own fault for not telling Lady Huntingdon that cream is wrong for me, Penelope told herself. But oh, dear God, don't let him hate me!'

★ ★ ★ ★

Lettice was not allowed at court; the sin of marrying Elizabeth's one love, Robert Dudley, Earl of Leicester, was one that the Queen would never forgive. So it was with Lady Huntingdon that Penelope set out next day, to Whitehall.

She made her curtsy to the Queen, very aware of her gorgeous gown, for a night's rest had laid *that* fear to rest; despite Lettice's words, she knew that the cream silk gown *was* gorgeous. Then she met her future husband. And they had barely exchanged more than a couple of sentences before another worry was put to flight. He did not hate her. Incoherent, mumbling, his face scarlet, it was obvious that he admired her very much indeed. And Penelope, smiling graciously at this slow-witted, powerfully built young man who was now Sir Robert Rich, did not wonder whether or not she hated him.

She did not yet know him. Perhaps further acquaintance would prove him to be endowed with the charm and kindliness which would make his plain, bulbous nosed face his only drawback as a husband. At least his open admiration meant that she was to be saved the humiliation she had felt when Philip Sidney had refused to consider marriage with her.

The weeks passed. She went to court, visited friends, had several more beautiful dresses made for her, and planned her wedding day. She gave little thought to the bridegroom for she did not see him often, and when she did he spoke so seldom that she felt they would never learn to know one another until they were married.

She gradually grew more at ease with her mother, and learned that Lettice was used to attracting men and did not much relish the fact that many of her one time swains now thronged around her daughter. Penelope soon began to trust in her own attractions a little more, too, for she had scores of admirers.

Summer began to fade, the colours glowing russet and gold instead of yellow and green. Penelope found herself with a trunk full of gowns and a rendezvous for marriage with a young lout of a man she still scarcely knew. She discovered he had a spiteful temper, and that his mind was slow compared with her own. He could not hold his drink, and was quick to blame others when at fault. Her little greyhound, Rebel, cringed away from him after an undeserved kick.

Penelope began to voice doubts, but Lettice scarcely pretended to listen. She did not find it amusing to have her beautiful daughter around the house, stealing the attention she felt was her due. She grew sharp and sarcastic when Penelope tried to reason with her, and Penelope saw their relationship threatened and sank back into believing it was merely Rich's impatience to be wed which had changed him. So one way and another, she went forward with her preparations complacently enough. Then she met Philip again, and in a moment, everything was different.

She and her mother had been shopping and on their return to Leicester House, Lettice had rushed up to the nursery to see her little Robbie. She was devoted to him, 'the child of my old age', as she jokingly called him, and though Penelope loved him as well she could not but wish she herself had reaped some of the wealth of affection with which Lettice showered her youngest son.

Bored with the chatter of Lettice's companion, the well-born but penniless Mistress Parry, Penelope wandered into the garden. In the late afternoon sunlight the herbs in the formal garden and even the low box hedges were giving off their perfume, all the sweeter for the touch of evening in the air.

Penelope strolled across the garden and pushed between the laden lavender bushes. She walked down the short flight of steps into the little orchard of plums and cherries.

It was pleasant in the orchard, but presently she walked down towards the river. There was always something to watch on the Thames; passing boats with court gallants and ladies aboard, wheeling gulls and kites, and the fishing boats bringing their cargo up to the great London fishmarkets.

She reached the screening willows which stood between the garden and the river, then realised she was not alone. A solitary figure stood close to the water's edge, a fishing rod in his hand. She opened her mouth to hail him, then closed it again. The man was not actually fishing, but was disentangling his line from the branch of an overhanging willow. Moving round cautiously, she at last saw his face; set at this moment, and frowning, whilst his fingers moved with neat, finicking movements and all his attention was given to his work.

She recognised Philip Sidney at once, but at that moment he gave an exclamation of satisfaction as his line was freed. He turned to ensure the line of his cast was clear, and saw her.

'I beg your pardon, lady,' he said politely, 'I am about to cast. If you could stand aside.'

'I thought you were the Earl of Leicester at first,' Penelope said. 'He often fishes from here. May I come down to the bank with you? Or perhaps I should be safer back at the house?'

He followed her glance at the willow which had recently been the cause of his annoyance, and laughed. 'I am not usually so maladroit,' he said. 'Come and stand by me.'

She joined him, stealing a laughing glance at his face, for she saw that he was puzzled, and too polite to ask her who she was.

'I am Sir Robert's stepdaughter, Penelope Devereux,' she said in answer to his unspoken question. 'And you are Sir Robert's nephew, Philip Sidney.'

She saw realisation fight with dazed disbelief, and her laughter rang out across the river, so that a lone fisherman on the far bank glanced across and smiled too.

'I've improved, haven't I?' she said. 'Judging by your expression I must have been a plain little girl.'

He began to protest, then smiled delightedly down at her. 'You were quite dreadful! But I should have guessed that your mother could not have produced anything but a beauty. You were at the ugly duckling stage, I suppose.'

She nodded, saying, 'Dotty, my younger sister, was always pretty, though. She never passed through any difficult, spotty stages, which seemed to me grossly unfair at the time.'

'Where have you been?' Philip said abruptly, and Penelope got the curious feeling that he'd not heard a word she had said.

'In York, mostly. With my guardians, Lord and Lady Huntingdon.'

'I knew you had not been at court, for if I'd seen you, I should not have forgotten,' Philip said simply. 'And why are you in London now, Mistress?'

And after all her dreams, she found it impossible to tell him. Instead, she shrugged and said evasively, 'My mother thought it time that I returned to her charge. Shall you be at court tomorrow, sir?'

He shook his head and fiddled with the rod, twisting it as though to find the best angle. 'No. The Queen has almost forgotten my indiscretion over the Alençon business, but it does not do to remind her by my continual presence.' He glanced down at Penelope, his mouth quirking. 'I daresay you know nothing of it, having been incarcerated in York at the time, but I disapproved of the French match which the Queen was toying with, and was foolhardy enough to say so and to write Elizabeth a letter, telling her what I thought.'

'I did hear,' Penelope said. 'She was very angry, wasn't she? Sir Robert has been in her black books too, for marrying my mother secretly. It is a credit to you both that you still have her Grace's favour. Limited favour, at any rate.'

He shrugged, his expressive face showing what he thought of the Queen's favour. 'I cannot say I crave for court life, for I do not. But for my uncle, it is different. The Queen and the court are his life. I mean no disrespect to Lady Leicester but no-one, no matter how dear, could make up to my uncle for estrangement from Elizabeth or politics. I am different. I enjoy country life, soldiering, what would you. With the right woman, rustication would be a pleasure.'

His words were straightforward, with none of the innuendo she had come to expect from young men. Yet she blushed.

'I had better go indoors now,' she said, abruptly aware that the sun had sunk below the horizon and that an autumnal chill was in the air. 'I want to see little Robbie before his nurse puts him to bed.'

She smiled, then turned and made her way back through the orchard. But before she mounted the steps to the formal garden she looked back. He was not fishing, nor was he watching her. He stood, head bent, apparently deep in thought. She felt a pang of disappointment that he had not followed her with his eyes, yet at the same moment thought that it was not with a woman's looks alone that Philip would fall in love.

And the thought comforted her, though she could not have said why.

FOUR

'I have never felt like this in my life before, Mary,' Philip said urgently. 'I scarcely dare to describe her, for you could not believe such perfection! I beg you to come to court, and meet her. You must love her, as I do.'

Mary glanced round at her pretty white and gold sitting room. She adored Wilton, and her son, and was very fond of her elderly husband. But to please Philip she would have done most things, and a sojourn in London was never dull, at any rate.

'I hope it is not just her beauty which attracts you,' Mary said. 'You have always despised men who fall in love with a pretty face, regardless of the mind behind it. Don't tell me, my dear, that you are mere human, like the rest!'

He smiled at the teasing note in her voice, but perfunctorily; where he felt strongly his sense of humour was apt to fail him.

'I've been staying with Uncle Robert and I've been in her company for three whole days,' he assured his sister. 'I admit that when she was a plain little girl I was blind to the mind behind the face. And now—well, I *am* dazzled, but not enough to mistake my heart. She is unaware of her own beauty, thinks herself no more than moderately good-looking, which is an attractive fault. She is ... unawakened describes her best.' He laughed, raising his brows in self-deprecation. 'Hear how I stumble when I speak of her, and I call myself a poet! But I love her, Mary, and always shall.'

He gazed into the fire which flickered on the hearth, dreaming of Penelope. Her quick mind, her gaiety, her innocent love of pleasure. Yet at the smallest word of criticism she would retire into her shell, her eyes downcast, her skin flushed.

He realised that Lettice neither loved the girl nor had the patience necessary to draw her out. He recognised and in a way understood the jealousy of a strikingly beautiful woman who sees herself compared, in men's eyes, with a young girl whose youthful bloom is at its height. He had seen, with his trained poet's eye, the difference between the two women's skin; Penelope's milky and smooth, her collar bones casting their little blue shadows, the line of her throat and jaw sharp and clean. And Lettice's skin was graining, the bones hidden beneath firm flesh, the line of her throat marred by a suggestion of sagging, the hint of a double chin.

Lady Leicester, he knew, with abnormal sensitivity, had known the comparison he was making without meaning to, and had made Penelope's evening miserable by the slight, disdainful comments she had passed on every word the girl had uttered.

'Strange, to think that she was offered to you in marriage when she was twelve,' Mary said, bringing him back to the reality of her sitting room at Wilton. 'I remember you wrote to me from Chartley, horrified that anyone should have expected such a sacrifice of you. "A mere child, and such a plain one, to share one's bed," you wrote.' She glanced up at him, her usually serious face alight with teasing. 'If I were her,

Philip, I'd make you suffer for that! She cannot have been ignorant of your feelings, I expect you made it plain enough that you'd no desire for her as a wife.'

'It was an indecency,' Philip said uncomfortably. 'Some women *are* ready for marriage young, but Penelope was not. Straight as a rod, skinny, with great big frightened eyes and a hunted look, as though she feared a beating.'

'Perhaps she got one, because you didn't want her,' Mary said, half laughing still, and was unaccountably worried when he said quietly, 'Perhaps she did.'

'I hope you are wrong; I wasn't serious,' Mary said. 'Is her mother strict with her? Or rather, was she strict when Penelope was a child?'

'Lettice never had the slightest interest in her children that I can remember,' Philip said slowly. 'It used to worry Walter. We were friends despite the differences in our ages and many times he spoke wonderingly of how a woman as passionate as his wife could regard her children so coldly. She was fonder of the boys, I believe, but even so one of Walter's last actions before he died was to make sure that she didn't get sole charge of any of their children.'

'Yet the last time Uncle Robert entertained my lord Pembroke, he came home vastly amused by the way the couple doted on little Robbie. He said Lady Leicester was quite besotted,' Mary said. 'However, Sir Walter could not have wished for more loving foster-parents than the Huntingdons. I'll wager they gave the little Devereux plenty of love.'

'You're right. But she's back with her mother now, and ...' he hesitated, then turned and faced his sister squarely. 'I beg you to come back to London with me, dearest. Lord Rich is dangling after her, and he's a wealthy man. I've not spoken to Penelope of my feelings for her, nor should I until I've had a word with Uncle Robert, and her mother. If you would come back with me, I feel that together we could convince everyone that I would make Penelope a good husband.'

'Of course I'll come,' Mary said. 'But I shall have to consult my dear lord before I rush off and leave him to fend for himself. I will come in three or four days. Will that do?'

★ ★ ★ ★

'I am not arguing with you, Letty. But the girl is a diamond of the first water, and it seems a pity to let Rich have her if she does not wish it. She might make an even better match.'

Robert Dudley stood behind his wife as she sat at her dressing-table, and smiled at her through the mirror with a certain amount of caution. He had already learned that to cross Letty could be dangerous, if not to life and limb, certainly to comfort.

But Letty, carefully darkening her eye-brows, merely said, 'She needs a man's hand to drive her, not mine! She needs marriage. And you know what a failure *my* marriage was! I chose for myself, a man who was handsome and charming and penniless. I might have been happy enough with Walter, if only we'd not had to scrimp and save and deny ourselves all the time. Believe me, Penny sees only that Rich is not handsome or exciting. But he has many virtues which will stand her in good stead once her romantic notions have worn off.'

'Be honest, Letty. His only virtue is money! I'm sure he will not be ungenerous to Penny but if she does not even like him very much now, would it not be better to let her wait for a few months? She may decide he is the right man for her, in the end.'

'The wedding is arranged and we are within four days of it,' Lettice said crisply. 'The groom can hardly keep his hands off her and suddenly the stupid chit starts to say she can't go through with it. She's had no chance to form an attachment for someone else, and in any case, the girl is almost pennilesss. Who else is likely to offer what Rich can?'

'As you say, she knows few young men; let me plead merely, as she does, for a little more time ...'

Lettice interrupted him. 'I had her stay here, Robert, so that she might marry Rich. Do you suppose the Huntingdons would take her back now, if she announced that she wanted more time to make up her mind? They would expect *me* to keep her here, have parties so that she might meet young men, investigate and bargain for a good match.'

Abruptly, she swung round on her stool and instead of her mirrored reflection, he saw her eyes, filled with tears, terribly vulnerable.

'Don't judge me too harshly, my darling,' she said. She got up from the stool and stood close to him, her arms encircling his waist, her body pressing close. 'It is not *fair*, not fair, that she should be so beautiful, and so young! It festers within me that I am growing old. Robert, I am forty! Whilst she is here, and your eyes are as hot upon her as the next man's, I cannot feel secure. If you love me, uphold me! She *must* marry Rich.'

As she finished speaking she pulled his head down to her own and as their lips met she pressed her body even closer, giving a sigh of satisfaction as she felt him respond. She could always rouse him and despite her fears and the subtle differences between glowing youth and middle age, he found her truly desirable, truly irresistible.

He reached for the strings of her negligee but she caught his hands and held them, laughing, already hot for him and wishful to end her resistance. 'Promise me that you will uphold my decision, that she *shall* marry Rich,' she said between her teeth.

He frowned, unwilling to submit to blackmail. 'Letty, foolish one! As though it makes any difference what I say! I don't see why Penny must marry at once, that is all! Give her until after the New Year celebrations and then, if she is still undecided, we will decide for her.'

She pulled away from him further, her face set. 'No!' she said violently. 'Why do you want her here for another month?' Suspicion entered her eyes, and her expression changed and became ugly. 'Do you want her for yourself, Robert? She is so young, so damned young!'

He saw her pain and knew a fleeting echo of it within his own breast. When he had seen Elizabeth flirting with Alençon, encouraging the wretched ape's pretensions, he had known jealousy so intense that he had, for the first time in his life, cast caution and self-interest to the winds. He had demanded of the Queen whether she now be maid or woman, and had taunted the ugly, pock-marked Frenchman. He loved Elizabeth in a totally different way from the way he loved his Letty, yet his recollection of his own tortured feeling for the Queen made it easier to understand Letty's passionate jealousy.

So he caught and held her, ignoring her breathless fury as she strove to withdraw the softness which he desired so much. 'Rightly were you called a she-wolf,' he said, smiling tenderly down into her furious and ashamed eyes. 'But nevertheless, I cannot have you believing me unfaithful, even in my thoughts. I swear it is not so; whilst I have you I need no other. Penny shall marry Rich as you have arranged. You must know what is best for your daughter.'

She relaxed against him, almost purring, her body responding and responsive under his hand. But even as he joyously claimed her, he felt a little stab of guilt. Sold for a romp with my own wife, he thought. But what right had I to interfere? None, of course. And he salved his conscience with the recollection of Rich's wealth and the beauty of the home to which he would take the girl.

★ ★ ★ ★

'The young people must leave us now,'
Lady Howard said authoritatively. 'Come,
Mary, Kate, it is the young women who
should help Lady Rich to prepare herself
for the marriage bed.'

Mary glanced around the big room,
already full of wedding guests who had
eaten well and drunk well and now waited
with impatience to see the bride bedded so
that they might continue with their own
pleasures.

'I will go with Penelope,' she said quietly,
and was pleased to see Kate Hastings nod
her head decisively. 'Perhaps she may find
an older woman can give her wiser council
now, than the young, unmarried girls.'

She caught Philip's eye over the heads of
the crowd as they left the room, and saw
his approving nod. He looked so wretched,
poor lad, she thought. When they had
reached London to find Penelope was to

marry Rich that very day she had thought he would go mad, but he had managed to contain his feelings and together, they had made their way to the church and later, to Leicester House, where the couple would spend this night.

Penelope, undressing in silence, looked as wretched as her brother, Mary thought, and as pale. Without a word she pulled off her embroidered silk stockings, her blue and silver garters, two or three elaborately worked petticoats. When she was standing in her shift, Mary pushed her down onto a stool and began to unpin her hair. Neatly untangling the flowers she had worn from the thick golden curls, she said in a low voice, 'Don't look so afraid, my dear. You will find that bedding is nothing to fear. Lord Rich is young, and will be gentle with you.'

'He is very angry with me,' Penelope said in a mutter. 'I tried to say I would not marry him—my mother and the Earl of Leicester had to force me into the church and I wept when he put the ring on my finger. I could hear him grinding his teeth when he took my arm, and he held it so tight that he bruised it.' She indicated her upper arm where the bruises had already showed black on the tender skin. 'I only hope he doesn't bear me a grudge still!'

'You are far too pretty to have a grudge borne against you,' Mary said gently. 'Don't let him think you fear him! Nothing is more liable to make a man angry, even when he has no right to be. I must leave you now. Hop into bed, child.'

'You are right, of course,' Penelope said. 'He is only a young man, and I've nothing to fear. It is just that ... that I don't know him very well, and ...'

'Into bed with you, or your man will be here,' interrupted a plump young woman with lascivious eyes. 'My, I envy you!'

Sitting up in bed with her long hair curling around her shoulders, and her face quite white, Penelope suddenly looked about twelve. Mary hesitated. Should she stay for a moment? But the door burst open and Robert Rich entered the room, pushed and jostled by the young bachelors who had accompanied him. He stopped, eyeing his bride with a mixture of greed and truculence which frightened Mary.

Then he turned and began to push his guests out of the room, laughing and shoving them, and Mary saw his round brown eyes and knew that, in his way, he was as apprehensive as his new wife.

As they made their way back to the main hall, Mary caught Lady Huntingdon's eye.

Kate said anxiously, 'I do hope Penelope will be all right. She is so *shy*, and Lord Rich is so ...'

Overhearing, another woman interrupted. 'They will be very much all right! What else should they be on their wedding night, pray?'

But the two older women could read the doubts in each other's eyes.

★ ★ ★ ★

'So we are married at last, eh Penny?'

'It would seem so, Robert.'

'No more foolish doubts then, my beauty? Never mind, I'll soon make you forget such nonsense. One woman is very much like another, I daresay.'

He guffawed, then pulled off his night-shirt and climbed into bed beside her. He put his hand on her breast and felt the shiver which ran through her. It roused him more than her kiss would have done, and he forgot all the lecturing he had endured from the Huntingdons, from old Burghley, even from Lord Leicester. 'Remember she is a gently bred girl, and knows nothing of men,' they had said. 'Remember that she is innocent.'

In the event, he remembered nothing, save how long he had waited, how much he wanted her.

He pushed her roughly onto her back, and tore off her shift without waiting to douse the candle. As he did so he saw her fear and it almost halted him, but the sight of her nakedness brought him to a point where he could think of nothing but possessing her.

When he had taken her he fell asleep almost at once, sprawled out on his back with his heavy arm flung across her stomach. Penelope lay still for a moment, then with the strength of revulsion, lifted up his arm and pushed it away from her. Her mind was numbed by her experience, but her body felt torn and bruised. Yet unexpected though the assault had been, she felt a kind of peace. Was that *all?* Toothache was as painful, and lasted much longer! She wished she had asked more questions about marriage, though. For instance, she lay here afraid to move her head on the pillow in case he woke and wanted to do it again. But she could not spend every night lying stock still in bed, so she had better make the experiment.

Cautiously, she moved her head so that

she could look at his face in the candlelight. God, but he was an ugly devil! But he was her fate, and she had better make the best of it.

She sat up carefully and doused the candle, but he stirred in his sleep and she lay back at once, her heart hammering.

She remembered Mary's advice, and thought perhaps she ought to blame herself, for her terror must have shown on her face. If she could bring herself to welcome him, perhaps he would be gentle. After all, she knew many, many woman married to men every bit as uncouth as Rich, and they seemed happy enough, so perhaps in time, she would find some pleasure in this strange business.

All of a sudden, she remembered the night she had gone to sleep in her mother's boudoir, and woken to find her mother and Sir Robert Dudley in the room. She had known, vaguely, that they were making love, but now she knew what they had been doing. And mother *enjoyed* it, she thought practically, remembering the murmurs and sighs she had heard.

But for me it has to be Robert Rich, she thought, and he is not the man I love. Then she was struck by an inspiration. I can pretend that it is someone else beside me, she thought. I can close my eyes and think that it is ... someone else.

Vaguely comforted by the thought that her mind at least was completely her own, a part of her that Robert Rich could not touch, she slept at last.

FIVE

'There it is, Penelope! Leighs, where our child will be born. Is it not beautiful?'

The rare enthusiasm in her husband's voice made Penelope look with even more interest at the scene before her.

A winding river valley, with the mist

just lifting from it and the rays of the spring sun bringing a delicate, almost ethereal beauty to the scene, was gradually revealed, like a stage curtain rising.

The old priory was crumbling away but its imposing stones still towered in a gatehouse and a great outer wall, left standing presumably to give added protection to the orchard which flourished in its shelter. Against the worn white stone, the rosy brickwork of modern Leighs looked a little raw, perhaps, but forty years had mellowed it, and already it had a look of cheerful permanence.

And the house was beautiful. Tall, twisted chimneys reared above a roof which was tiled, and the tiles were golden lichened in places, adding to the feeling of age. Timbers glowed a pale, clean silvery colour and the windows were wide and so placed that they gave the house a cheerful, frank appearance.

As they approached, detail sprang to the eye. Another piece of priory work was the well in the courtyard, with its pinnacled roof and the conduit leading out of it. She saw that the tiles of the courtyard were many coloured, and guessed that they had come from the priory too, but how delightful they looked, sparkling in the spring sunshine, instead of being forever shaded by a roof!

In the doorway, the dowager Lady Rich waited to welcome her to her new home. Penelope dismounted from her horse and watched whilst the groom ran out of the stables and took the reins; then she walked slowly towards Rich's stepmother.

'So this is your new wife, Robert,' Catherine Rich said briskly. She pecked Penelope's cheek, then stood aside to let her enter. 'I believe you are pregnant, so I must hope you had an uneventful journey.'

Assuring her that the ride down had been delightful, Penelope surreptitiously studied the other woman. After all, Catherine Rich could make a great difference to her life here at Leighs. If she refused to surrender the reins of the house to her daughter-in-law they might spend bitter months in wrangling. On the other hand, her co-operation could perhaps mend Penelope's shaky marriage.

She saw a handsome, determined looking woman, perhaps eight or ten years her senior. Dark haired, with very light blue eyes, and a nose which barely escaped being dubbed roman, she seemed to Penelope to be an ally well worth the winning.

As they climbed the stairs, Penelope said rather timidly, 'You are very young, Lady Rich. I had imagined that you would be much older! But I hope we may be friends whilst we share this roof.'

'I am sure we will, for I've no desire to oust you from your place as mistress,' the other said frankly. 'You must call me Catherine, as Robert does, for as you say, we are much of an age. Until you are used to the servants and Robert's ways, I will order the household, but you must then begin to take over from me. I have every intention of marrying again, you see, for the single state would not suit me. The late Lord Rich left me well provided for, but I want children of my own, not other women's brats.' She looked quickly at Penelope. 'That was not meant as a dig at you, Penelope. But I have mothered Robert and his sisters to the best of my ability since my marriage. It is time I had children of my own.'

They entered a room, furnished in pale green with the fourposter bed dominating it. 'This is the main bedroom,' Catherine said. 'I moved out as soon as Robert married you, and have a smaller room at the back of the house. You will find this room is warm and pleasant; it faces the courtyard, which means it is more sheltered than the rooms on the outer walls of the house, and the view is very pretty. You can see the church, and the river, and you can watch what goes on in the courtyard if you are confined to your room for a while, after the child is born.'

Penelope said gratefully, 'It is a beautiful room, and I wish I had not turned you out. But it is the way of the world, is it not? Will you go to London to find a husband, or are your family arranging a match?'

'Both,' Catherine said promptly. 'I shall remain here for a year, and then I shall join my family in London. I do not intend to marry another old man, be he never so rich!' She laughed at the unintentional play on words and Penelope laughed with her.

Behind them, Rich's voice said heavily, 'May anyone share the joke?'

They swung round, and Penelope said immediately, 'How could anyone be un-happy at Leighs, Robert, for it is so beautiful! And Catherine has made me feel very welcome.'

'I daresay,' Robert said sulkily. 'But I should show you the house and grounds, not her. Come, Penny, take off your hat and I'll show you everything!'

Catherine gave her a little push and

she went to him at once, smiling and gay. Even after four months of marriage she was afraid of his violent outbursts of temper, when he would hit her for a trifle, a word. Yet she had early found that what annoyed him worst was her fear so she tried to dissemble, but she could not prevent the involuntary wince away from his hand, bringing her the very blows she tried to avoid.

As she followed him, admiring and exclaiming, she thought of the past four months. They had been made endurable because Philip had remained in London, always near at hand. She hungered for the sight of him, yet the sight of him was sufficient. She basked in his admiration, the tones of his deep, thoughtful voice calmed her worst moments, yet she did not desire to carry their friendship any further. She behaved coquettishly when in his company because it was expected of a young and attractive married woman, but she expected him to behave with decorum towards her, and a display of ardour would have frightened her as much as it would have repelled her.

For she valued their friendship above all things, and how, she asked herself, could she have remained his friend if he had tried to fall upon her as Rich did, mauling, insistent, insulting and violating with his desires the delicate privacy of her tender flesh.

Philip had seemed to know instinctively, that she wanted only his friendship. And even when they had met, that last day in London, to say goodbye, he had done no more than clasp her hand, his eyes eloquent.

'You will bear your child at Leighs then, Lady Rich?' he said. 'May I bring my sister, Lady Pembroke, to visit you?' He looked around him, then lowered his voice. 'Forgive me, perhaps I should not mention it, but I feel I must. Will Lord Rich take advantage of the loneliness of Leighs to ill-treat you further? I have noticed ... I could not help noticing ...'

She cut across his diffident words, saying 'I must learn to manage my husband, Sir Philip. Perhaps I can best do it when we have only each other to mind. And please do bring Mary down to visit me, it would be delightful.'

'I'm sorry,' he said at once, accepting the rebuke. 'Goodbye, Lady Rich.'

He bent to kiss her hand and as his lips met her skin the oddest thing happened. The child within her moved, a feeling so totally unexpected and strange that she cried out.

Philip raised his eyes to her face. 'What is it?'

'The baby—it moved!' she said, and felt once again the gentle flutter within her, as though the child was a bird, trying its wings for the first time. 'Oh, what a wonderful feeling!'

Her face must have been a mirror for her emotions, for he smiled at her with tenderness, then patted her hands gently before releasing them. Dazed with the wonder of it, the sudden feeling of closeness with the life within her, she moved away from him.

Of course, the baby would be with her, wherever Rich might take her. It would be hers in a way nothing had ever been before.

The two of us are strong enough for anything, she said to herself, and meant it.

★ ★ ★ ★

As the weeks passed, Penelope's understanding of her husband grew. She discovered that much of his bad-temper and brutality sprang from a basic insecurity. He was not quick, in fact he was slow-witted, and his father had not prepared him for the place he was to take. The affairs of the estate worried him, money matters confused him, and figures were the bane of his life. She saw that he hit out not only at her but at the servants, and often his rage was not over their incompetence or slowness, but over his own, which he could not acknowledge.

Slowly, she began to help him. At first she just took over the books, saying that she wanted to be useful and she might as well save his time for him. Then, she began to pay the wages, to query some of the expenditure, to plan the servants' tasks so that they had spare time to amuse themselves yet were fully occupied at other times.

He became easier to live with, less aggressive. As Penelope's stomach continued to swell she began to congratulate herself upon her handling of the marriage. She would never love him, but at least they could share a happy enough life.

Oddly enough, what set the seal on this early contentment was the ruthless command of an elderly aunt of Robert's, Aunt Isabel. She came to stay with them when Penelope was six months pregnant and having thoroughly taken to her new niece, proceeded to lay down the law to her nephew.

'No more lovemaking, Robert, until after the child is born,' she said fiercely. 'Understand, boy? I've no doubt that Catherine will uphold me that such carryings-on are natural before a child is conceived. But at this stage your wife must be left alone, to make the baby. No interfering, Robert. You tell me, Penelope, if he puts your child at risk.'

Penelope, convulsed with silent mirth at the look of fascinated horror on Rich's face, hurried to her room and threw herself on the bed, giggling helplessly. And later, when he sought her bed, she reminded him of the old lady's words with some enjoyment. But presently, to her surprise, she found that she missed him. She began courting him, smiling into his eyes when they were in company, standing close to him, catching his hand and holding it on her stomach so that he, too, could feel their child moving.

And when he put his arms round her one night and drew her close, breathing of how he wanted her, he was not repulsed. Instead he found her eager, and for the first time their pleasure was shared, doubling the enjoyment for them both.

When the long awaited visit of the Countess of Pembroke came, Penelope was unaware that she had visitors. Catherine Rich had welcomed them and sent a servant to fetch Penelope, but the servant went to the pleasure gardens, and Penelope had been visiting the farm. She walked into the parlour, hair loose, gown loose, face shining with perspiration from her energetic walk, to find Mary sitting smiling at her, and Philip on his feet, his eyes full of affection.

She exclaimed, apologising for her untidiness, but Philip gestured her to a chair, saying 'Nonsense, Lady Rich, you are in splendid looks! Pregnancy and the country both suit you, that's plain!'

She smiled and agreed that the country suited her, and then conversation became general. But Penelope was aware that Philip's eyes never left her, even when he was giving his opinion at length upon the newest addition to Mary's stable, a strawberry roan mare of showy good looks but no performance.

Mary and Catherine were talking recipes, and Catherine jumped to her feet and suggested they adjourn to the kitchen, so that she could show Lady Pembroke the great cake which cook was even now icing.

'And you must come to the stable with me, Lady Rich, so that you can see Mary's poor horse, and the magnificent beast which bore me here,' Philip said. 'You have probably not seen a horse like mine before—she's a mare, actually. I had her imported—but come!'

He held out his hand and she hesitated only a moment, then allowed him to take her arm.

'Robert will be back from the fields soon,' she told him as they walked across the stableyard. 'He will be happy to see you and your sister.'

There was no possibility of being alone with Philip, nor did Penelope wish it. The house was full of servants, as were the stables. But she found herself much more excited by Philip's nearness than she had previously been. When he touched her arm she felt a spine-tingling awareness which was half pleasurable, half frightening. But even as she met his eyes and acknowledged his attraction she was equally aware of her baby; of its small, sleepy movements, and of its complete dependency upon her.

Whilst I carry the child, she mused, I can be no more than half-interested in anything else, for with the other half of my mind I am concentrating upon my baby, absorbed in the creation of new life.

However, they could talk more freely here than in the parlour with Mary and

Catherine listening.

'Do you miss London, and court?' asked Philip.

The words were straightforward enough, but she caught the implication of his own presence in London, and answered both the spoken and unspoken query.

'I shall miss it more, perhaps, when my baby is born,' she said. 'But at the moment I am so busy, learning to keep house, making clothes for my baby, helping my husband with the books. Having a baby is a very enthralling thing. All one's thoughts and feelings are bound up with the child, and other things become less significant. I feel the need for peace and quiet, and God knows, there is peace and quiet in plenty at Leighs!'

'But afterwards?'

She laughed. 'That, I fear, will be a different story. I shall need London and my friends again, once the birth is behind me.'

'Do you fear it?'

'No. Why should I? It is natural, and I don't fear nature.'

He nodded, and stood aside for her to enter the stable. Inside a groom polishing harness nodded to them, and Philip walked down the rows of stalls until he came to his mare.

'Come my sweetheart, come up, my honey,' he crooned, backing the horse out of the stall. 'Is she not a beauty? See the lines of her, the turn of her head. And she moves with such gaiety.'

'She is a fine creature,' Penelope acknowledged. 'What a strange colour, but altogether delightful.' She laughed. 'Why, she is a little like me, she has creamy gold hair and dark eyes! What do you call her?'

'Wintersweet, and her foal will be called Jasmine.'

'Is she carrying? She shows no sign of it.'

'She may not be,' admitted Philip with a grin. 'Contrary creature that she is! She was covered by a magnificent stallion of my own breeding, though, so I am hoping.'

'Pregnancy all around you,' Penelope said with a smile. 'Myself, the size of a house, your sister Mary growing daily, and even your horse carries more than meets the eye.'

'The state suits you all,' Philip said gallantly. He led the mare back into the stall and rejoined Penelope so that they stood for a moment, side by side, contemplating the mare.

Nothing could have been more innocent, but Robert Rich, entering the sunny yard with his led horse breathing into his collar and almost treading on his heels in its eagerness to get into its stall, was startled by the sight of the two motionless figures. So was his horse, for it bucked and gave an earsplitting neigh and Penelope, thoroughly startled, jumped and clutched Philip.

Philip, with great presence of mind, went at once to the horse's head, soothing and fondling whilst he said gently, 'We startled your horse, I'm afraid, Rich. I've been showing your wife my Spanish mare—see her there, in the stall? She is the only one of her kind in England I believe. They call these yellow horses Isabellas in Spain, and in France they are Palominos. This one is in foal I believe, the sire is a light chestnut, and I hope to get a yellow foal out of her. She's a first-class beast, and should produce for several years yet. What do you think?'

Rich glanced with glowering suspicion from Philip's earnest countenance to Penelope's interested one. 'Run indoors,' he said peremptorily to his wife. 'Stables and horses are men's business. Is it possible to buy one of these Spanish mares and have it imported, Sidney? The colour is remarkable—it matches Penny's thatch! I wouldn't mind adding a mare like that to my stable!'

Penelope left the two men discussing the possibility of obtaining a palomino mare for Rich, and rejoined Mary and Catherine, now back in the parlour.

'I think I will change my dress before we dine,' she said apologetically to the two women. 'You must have thought me very remiss, Mary, not to have changed before, but in the excitement of seeing you I forgot my appearance. I shall not be long.'

Going across the hall she met Rich, who said that he, too, wanted to change out of his working clothes.

Making their way up the stairs and along the corridor, Rich chatted pleasantly, so that Penelope was all the more amazed by the storm which broke when they entered their room. Lavender was there, with a jug of hot water, a clean gown spread out on the bed, and a flask of scent ready to dab on her mistress's brow and wrists. It was early and no candles were lit, but a fire crackled on the hearth and the room presented a familiar and cosy appearance.

Rich changed all that.

'Out!' he said to Lavender, and when

she began to remonstrate, bundled her through the door himself with such force that she fell onto the shining boards. Before she could pick herself up he had closed the door and shot the heavy bolt across. Then he turned to Penelope.

'Why were you in the stables with Sidney?' he said. And whilst surprise still held her dumb he added, 'And why did you jump apart, like guilty lovers, when I surprised you?'

Frightened by his darkening countenance and quite unable to see any reason for his obvious rage, Penelope said 'I had gone to see the yellow mare, as Sir Philip told you. I jumped because of the way your horse screamed—it sounded as though someone was being murdered behind me! And if you think, sir, that I would sink to conducting a sordid affair in a stable under the eye of the grooms, and in *my* condition, then your opinion of my morals and intelligence must be low indeed!'

He began to answer her, and she saw

that he knew her to be innocent and had merely been thrown into a rage by something else. Indignation that she should be the butt of such accusations just so that he could punish someone made her bold, and she glared at him, then turned away with something perilously like a sneer on her lips.

Rich strode across the room and pulled her round to face him. 'How dare you doubt my morals and intelligence!' he shouted. 'Why, I've been faithful to you—'

He broke off and before either of them had had time to consider his words, he had hit her full across the face.

She stood, swaying from the blow, her eyes searching his face. 'I didn't mean *your* morals,' she began, and then something in his demeanour gave her the clue.

She had heard rumours of a woman he visited on the estate, and had thought little of it. After all, he did not bring the wench to the house nor mention her before his wife. And since she did not love him she did not think it right to deny him the other woman's company.

This, then, was the answer. Rich's woman had denied him, in a moment of bravado, had sent him to the rightabout. And in his rage he had turned on her, his lawful wife, thinking if he could not beat his mistress, then he would take it out on the mother of his child!

'How dare you hit me,' she said, in a whisper. 'I know why, though! It is because of Meggie, isn't it, Robert. You are hitting me because you can't hit her!'

'What do you know of Meggie? I don't know what you mean,' he blustered. His colour came up like a tide, dying his face scarlet. 'You called me immoral, you stupid bitch!'

He hit her again, knocking her back against the wall, then jumped at her, grabbing her by her long loose hair. He pulled it back until her eyes were watering with the pain of it, but she made no attempt to escape, she just curled her hands round her stomach and never took her eyes off his face.

'It is *you* who are immoral,' he insisted. He gave her hair another jerk, and smiled as the tears which she could not hold back rolled down her pale cheeks. 'If you ever look at another man I'll pull every hair from your head, until you look like a nun, even if you won't act like one. Remember that!'

He released her and she still did not speak, but he could read the sick disgust in her eyes. He pushed his face into hers, wanting more than anything to wipe that look off her face, to have her crying, pleading; anything but looking at him so coldly, as though she could see through him to his very soul, and what she saw was infinitely distasteful.

But her eyes were steady and she did not answer him or look away. He hit her again, a double buffet across the head, and she sagged, slowly collapsing against the wall and onto the floor. He dragged her up, seeing her eyes only half-conscious, but the disgust in them still undimmed.

In a frenzy he threw her onto the bed and flung himself after her. She pulled her legs up and tried to curl into a ball but he was beyond reasoning, and would not allow himself to see how she was trying to protect her unborn child. She was frustrating him, and that was enough.

He tore at her gown and then, suddenly, she came alive again and began to fight, her eyes wild, her cries coming at last, because she knew what he meant to do.

His fury would not be denied, and in the end, she was powerless to stop him. Afterwards, he left her, moaning and sick, to make her apologies to her guests. She was ill, he said, and would be unable to dine with them.

Lavender crept into the bedroom, and wept to see her mistress's bruised and battered body. She brought Catherine, who acted sensibly, bathing the younger woman's hurts and bringing her nourishing broth.

But her ministrations came too late, the damage was done. During the hour before dawn, after what felt like a lifetime of suffering, Penelope gave birth to a dead child.

The next day Rich visited his wife, penitent as a dog who had done wrong and knows it, but does not relish a beating. He looked into her eyes, which once had been so full of generosity for him, and read unyielding bitterness there. She would never forgive him. Even his tears did not move her. He apologised, abased himself, swore to treat her like a queen in future, and her countenance remained unchanged. She was pale and drawn from her labour, but he knew she could have smiled at him had she wished.

He sat by her bedside for a long time, and he learned a lot of things. He learned that she would never fear him again, and would protect herself against him by some means or other, and he learned that he had lost her before he had ever really possessed her.

He tried, for the first time in his life, to explain to her about the feelings which came to him when he could *not* understand, when he saw that even his servants smiled at his slowness. And at last, she signified that she understood, but that he must leave her now, to regain her strength.

Cold and alone, but not so cold and alone as she, he sought comfort at last, in sleep.

SIX

The candles guttered in their holders as the draught caught them yet again, slipping between the velvet hangings and making the flames curtsy. Penelope frowned, and moved the sheet before her so that the light fell steadily upon it once more. She was reading a poem, and it was a poem which brought a flush to her cheeks, because it was dedicated to her.

After her miscarriage, Rich had not tried to stop her returning to London. Indeed, because of the loss of the child, she had found her freedom. Rich had changed, but he was still a violent man, who would beat her if he did not dread the revenge she would take. For her revenge had been simple, and immediate. She had moved into a room of her own and when he displeased her, she locked her door against him. Never again, she told him, would she allow his desires or hers to give him power over her.

She entertained whom she wished now, either in her London lodgings or at Leighs. Philip was a frequent visitor. She supposed people thought he came to visit her husband but she no longer cared what anyone thought. Why should she? The Queen did not like her, so she only went to court when it suited her to do so. Her life was very much her own.

She read the last line of the poem and sighed with pleasure. What beautiful words, bringing to life beautiful thoughts and feelings. He wanted her, she knew *that* without reading his poetry. But she would not sell her body into slavery for any man, not she! She was sure that Philip would not mistreat her, but she had no desire to re-awaken appetites in her which she knew must stay suppressed. When she allowed Robert to make love to her, she detached her mind from the experience. Indifference, with wariness against possible pain, was her best defence.

And Philip was coming to her now, as he had come so many times in the past few months. She could picture him striding through the dark streets. He would be wary, for attacks on solitary gentlemen were not uncommon, but he would accept the risk gladly, for was it not good for a poet to stride through danger to reach his heart's desire?

She imagined his face, its beauty reflecting his soul. The grave glance, which could change to mirror delighted amusement or soften to reveal a depth of tenderness not normally associated with soldiers—for soldier he was, amongst other things.

She laid the poem down and turned to her dressing-table. Her mirrored face looked back at her; serene, more beautiful in the faint candle glow than it was in reality. She was wearing a loose gown, a pretty, delicate thing in powder-blue. She unfastened it at the throat, then lower, so that the valley between her breasts could be faintly discerned between the ruffling lace.

She wondered whether, tonight, they would become lovers. Then she shrugged, impatient with herself. After all, neither of them had hurried their relationship, except, perhaps in verse. When the time was ripe for them, they would know it.

Leaning forward, she rang the bell on the dressing-table vigorously and strolled from her bedroom into the small boudoir next door when she entertained her women friends.

Lavender came quickly through the door.

'I was in the parlour, making up the fire milady,' she said. 'Are you coming through now?'

'No. I shall entertain Sir Philip in here,' Penelope said nonchalantly. 'Bring him in, Lavender, and then you may retire to bed.'

'Not before you go, madam,' Lavender said, pursing her mouth. 'Who will undress you, braid your hair?'

Her eyes met Penelope's and she read their message.

'Oh, no, milady,' she said, shocked. 'Why, that is not at all how you were brought up. Your mother would be very distressed.'

'My mother,' Penelope said with dis-interested finality, 'Sleeps with her master of horse. And she slept with the Earl of Leicester whilst my father lived. Don't quote *her* to me as an example of purity, for I know better. Do as I say, Lavender.' She waited until the woman was bending over, filling the hearth with logs from the basket, before adding, 'Besides, it may never happen.'

'That's true, you may think better of it,' Lavender said. She dusted her hands on her apron and clucked at the smears of woodash. 'There, madam, look what you've made me do! But this can be washed out, and all as clean as before.' She spoke with emphasis and Penelope, vastly amused by the analogy, gave a snort of laughter. 'Aye, well, you may laugh,' Lavender said darkly. 'But what you've given, you can't take back, and when a loaf is cut, there's no making it whole again.'

'I've already given, and my loaf is

definitely cut,' Penelope said. 'Now if I say a watched pot never boils and a stitch in time saves nine, you may consider this conversation at an end! Go downstairs now, there's a kind Lavender! Sir Philip will be at the door soon enough, and I'd rather you let him in and brought him up than one of the servants who does not have my confidence.'

She watched the woman close the door carefully behind her, then turned back to the mirror. 'I am twenty years old,' she told herself. 'I've never been in love, never born a living child. It is time I did both, before lines come on my face and my hair turns white.' Then she laughed, because she could not imagine herself in any way different from the way she was now, at this moment. Sitting in the candlelight, with her skin smooth and clear and her hair spilling over her shoulders like cloth of gold, waiting for her lover.

★ ★ ★ ★

Philip strode along the dark, ill-lit street, avoiding the kennel. Rain sluiced, sweet and cold, down the sides of his face, a diamond drop hung from his nose, his lashes were bearded with moisture. When he passed a big house with light streaming from the front windows he saw that his shadow, black and splendid as it climbed the housefront opposite and then slid down onto the puddled cobbles, was of a young man whose curls were sleeked to his head like a seal.

He did not mind the rain; in fact, he was enjoying it. It damped down the abominable London street smells, drove the idle beggars and the sly gutter-children indoors, and made the walk from his father's house to the Rich lodgings an adventure.

Boylike, he imagined himself the captain of a ship; the rain which drove into his face was not rain but spray, the cobbles which slipped beneath his feet were the boards of a tipping, treacherous deck. He smiled at himself, but continued the game until suddenly, his thoughts turned to Frances Walsingham.

Here he was, going to see the most beautiful woman in London, going with a poem, fresh written to her loveliness, in his pocket. And yet his father and the Queen's secretary, Sir Francis Walsingham, were arranging a marriage between him and Walsingham's thin and solemn child, who loved him already, they said.

He turned the corner by instinct, almost, so well did he know the way. A crazily tipping house, the top storey four feet into the road, suddenly deluged a guttering shower down his neck, but he shrugged it away and walked on. Frances Walsingham! A nice child, a young woman almost, for she must be nearly fifteen. But his wife? He tried to imagine his hands on her young, obedient body, and blushed.

He remembered Mary's words; kindly, a little censorious.

'You do not have to tell me that Penelope is not your mistress; that is not the point, the point is that you love her and want her,' she said. 'But a man needs a *wife*, Philip! Frances is not too young and if you do not take her, another will. She is young and strong and of good family, and she will be generously dowered. She is fond of you and rather pretty. You cannot have Lady Rich, so why not take Frances?'

'Looks do not matter to me,' Philip said coldly, and saw Mary try to hide a smile.

Now, in the wet and windy darkness, he tried to set the mental image of Frances beside that of Penelope, and failed. Frances, poor child, was not memorable enough for that game. He knew she was dark haired, small and neat.

And Penelope? He pictured her as he had seen her last, in a white gown with primroses embroidered on it, her splendid figure showing even through the bonings and paddings of her dress, her shining hair defying the attempts to frizz it into ugliness, those startlingly black eyes gazing frankly at him.

Carried away by his thoughts, he trod in a puddle or worse, judging by the horrible squelch which almost brought his boot off his foot as he pulled himself clear. That is what comes of day-dreaming, he scolded himself. You'll end up confronting your mistress with a smell so strong on you that she'll be forced to order your dismissal!

He loved her so intensely that the humour of the situation was lost on him; he was truly concerned that Penelope might be offended by him. For he was now lamentably wet and muddy; he could feel the damp across his shoulders so the rain had penetrated cloak, doublet and shirt, and he could see even in the poor light from passing windows that he was mired to the knee.

But at last he was in her road, beneath her very windows. He wiped his wet face with his wet sleeve and sniffed, then hammered on the door. Just as it began to open he bethought himself of his handkerchief but before he could find it in the entanglement of wet cloak, wet gloves and cold fingers, Lavender was beckoning him inside.

'She's in the sitting room,' the woman observed, adding with concern, 'Why, you're terribly wet, sir. But there's a good fire upstairs; you'll soon dry out. I'll take your cloak.'

Impatient, he ran up the stairs and then had to wait whilst Lavender toiled up behind him, breathing heavily.

She knocked on the door, swinging it inwards as she did so, announcing, 'Sir Philip Sidney to see you, milady!'

He entered the room and shut the door behind him, then leaned on it, the better to take in the vision before him. She had risen as he entered and now stood quite still, her hair hanging loose, her eyes fixed on his.

'You're soaked,' she said at last, and

he thought her voice trembled. 'Come to the fire.'

He approached the fire, miserably conscious that he squelched with every step. He *ached* to touch her, but made no attempt to do so. He had touched her hand, her shoulder in the past, and had felt her shrink.

And he was so wet! She was standing close to him now, looking almost anxiously up into his face. She said in a husky whisper, 'Your hair is dark with water,' and put her hand on his brow, smoothing back the soaked lock which had fallen over his eyes.

The movement had brought her closer still so that they were almost touching. He swallowed. Damn it, it was an invitation! He simply could not hold back a moment longer, even if he frightened her and lost his chance. He pulled her into his arms and bent his head, to kiss her lips for the first time. She felt so soft and pliable! With a jerk of astonishment he realised that beneath her loose gown she must be naked, or he would have felt the bones of her bodice beneath his fingers instead of the suppleness of her back.

He felt her pull away and released her at once, smiling down at her, knowing that their moment had come and that she knew it as well as he.

'Take your wet things off,' she said, smiling at him in return, her eyes mirroring the desire which he knew must be in his own. 'You are cold now, but you will soon be warm.'

She led him through the door into the adjoining room where, without self-consciousness, she threw off her loose gown. He found himself scrambling out of his clothes, furious with his cold fingers which would not do as he told them, so fastenings almost defeated him. She laughed and helped him, promising him again that he would not be cold for long.

When they were both naked they tumbled into bed and she caught his icy fingers and thrust them between the warm silk of her thighs. He felt the keenness of his love mingle with desire so that it was like pain, stabbing at his heart, shortening his breath. For a moment he lay still, marvelling at this thing which had happened to them, then he was upon her, rejoicing in her eagerness, accepting with gratitude and tenderness this gift of herself which she so generously bestowed.

★ ★ ★ ★

'You have changed, you know, Penny. Such a funny, shy, awkward little creature you were when we were children. And then when you were first married you still seemed shy and you let everyone push you around. It is only now that you've blossomed out into the sort of sister any man would be proud of! God, you're the toast of the court, d'you know that? Everyone is writing poetry to Lady Rich, Philip Sidney is head over ears in love with you, and even the Queen is curious to see this lady who is so lovely that you're known as "Stella" because you are a star of perfection!'

Robert, Earl of Essex, very much the man about town, leaned on his sister's desk in her little study at Leighs, and smiled beguilingly down at her.

Penelope laid down her pen and smiled back.

'My dear, you are quite my favourite brother and I've always loved you for your charm and truthfulness, but why are you trying to woo me now? You are at court, high in her Grace's favour, yet you visit me in the country. There has to be a reason!'

'Well, I'm not very much at court *yet,*' Essex reminded her. 'But I do want to be! I am taken about by our stepfather, who is training me for a similar position to that held by him. The thing is, Penny, that it would interest the Queen to see you again (she says she can't recall much about you from previous meetings, apart from your yellow thatch!), and it might do me some good to introduce you.'

'I see. Well, Essex, I might as well be frank with you. I have my little girls to look after here, but I must admit I hanker for the court, or for London life, at any rate. But Sidney has married his Frances, and I felt it would be better if I rusticated here for a while.'

'You mean until you had regained your looks after the birth of the latest brat,' Essex said without rancour. 'Well, you seem as beautiful as ever to me! As for Frances, she is a plain little thing. Do come back to London with me, Penny! You shall have your suite of rooms at Leicester House, they are always kept ready for you—they are even called Lady Rich's rooms. How about it?'

Penelope sniffed. Just before Philip's wedding she had visited the court, half to see her rival but ostensibly to try to undo the harm the impetuous Dorothy had done to the name of Devereux in the Queen's eyes.

For Dotty had eloped with a young man called Thomas Perrot, and the scandal had been such that Elizabeth had practically banned the entire family from her presence. Lettice, furious with her daughter and bitterly blaming herself for the girl's wildness, had implored Penny to go to court and to explain to anyone who would listen that she and Leicester were as distressed as anyone.

She had seen Lord Burghley who had said frankly that at least with Dorothy married Lord Leicester would be unable to plot any more madness with James of Scotland. He had been only half-serious, but Penelope had heard of the Queen's fury when it was revealed that Leicester had tried to marry off the youngest Devereux daughter to King James, and thought privately that there was a great deal in what he said.

She knew, and suspected Burghley did

too, that Leicester was now hoping to bring about a marriage between Arabella Stuart and Essex, but she knew her brother. He would not willingly tie himself down in marriage to a female of little beauty and fewer brains, unless he was convinced that to do so was to his advantage. And judging by the things the Queen was apt to say about Arabella, whoever married the girl would not be in prime favour at court!

And then, as she strolled through the privy chamber with Burghley at her side, she had seen Philip. He was sitting on the arm of a chair, chatting to a demure young woman in a neat fawn gown, he looked up, and when he saw her there was no denying the undoubted pleasure which brought a flush to his thin cheeks. He jumped to his feet and called her over, introducing the girl as 'Mistress Walsingham, my betrothed'.

Frances smiled politely and got to her feet. Penelope saw that she was small and slim with pansy brown eyes set in a lively little face and a mouth whose lips were held in rather a tight line. Her figure was slight, lacking the curves of womanhood which would come with the years.

She murmured a few socially correct remarks, and then Frances looked fully at her for the first time. 'She knows,' Penelope thought, and felt pleased that the other could detest her so thoroughly, for it was a sign that she acknowledged Penelope's power over Philip.

But go back to London with Essex? She thought of seeing Philip again and her heart gave a great lurch of pleasure. But would she be strong enough to deny him, if he came to her?

Abruptly, she made up her mind. What was the point of hiding away in Essex? She would have to return to London one day, and see Philip and young Lady Sidney.

'I'll come,' she told her brother, and was rewarded by his dazzling smile. 'You'd best send a messenger to Leicester House so that my arrival doesn't put mother out.'

'She's expecting you,' Essex said with a smirk. 'My powers of persuasion are famous already, you know! Neither of us really thought that you'd refuse.'

And laughing indulgently, thinking how charmingly Essex had turned from boy to man, Penelope went to pack.

★ ★ ★ ★

'What a house party I shall have!' Lettice said amiably as she and Penelope settled down with their work in the parlour at Leicester House. 'Your brother is here, and keeps bringing maids of honour (a misnomer, that) to see me; your sister and her dreadful husband are coming in a day or two, and baby Walter, who is a big lad now and no mistake, is with the Earl and will be returning here in an hour or two. Oh, and so is his nephew, Philip Sidney, whom I believe you know.'

She smiled with malicious meaning at her daughter, who smiled back demurely, but did not answer.

'Your husband is not with you,' Lettice remarked after a moment. 'Why is that? Doesn't he like us?'

'He doesn't like London,' Penelope said. 'Any more, apparently, than Lady Sidney does. Or is she staying here too, with her husband?'

'She is at Barn Elms, with her mother and her daughter Fanny,' Lettice said promptly. 'A charming young woman, I believe?'

'I scarcely know her,' Penelope replied.

Their talk moved on, then, to other things, but at least her curiosity had been satisfied. Fond though Philip might be of Frances, they were not inseparable. She must wait now, and see how marriage had changed him.

★ ★ ★ ★

They met that evening, at dinner. Penelope thought that Philip had scarcely changed at all at first, but gradually, she saw that he had. He had always been serious but now he was more so, his smile came seldom and shone briefly on his face.

After the meal he drew her apart and they talked quietly whilst around them the family bickered and laughed, seeming for a moment, thought Penelope, like any ordinary family group rather than the estranged, uncaring people that circumstances had made out of them.

'So little love was given us, as children, that we find it difficult to give love in our turn,' she said to Philip. 'And we've no true sense of family, as you and Robert and Sir Henry have. We spent too many years apart, or fighting for a share of mother's attention. Not Essex, of course. He was her favourite, and got everything he desired. But Dotty and I, and baby Walter.'

'Yet you never seemed jealous of your brother.'

'Jealous? Good Lord, no! We loved him

devotedly, Dotty and I, and he loved us. With me, particularly, he would share everything he had, he was so generous and sweet! He would even try to draw me into the charmed circle of mother's love—with little success, alas! I was not the sort of child my mother felt she deserved! And I looked after him when she was absent, tried to see that he wanted for nothing in the way of affection at least.'

'Which is why he is so self-confident; and so abominably spoilt,' Philip remarked. 'But his charm makes one forget all that. And now stop all this small-talk, you adorable creature. When may I come to you?'

She felt the excitement bring blood hot to her cheeks, but she said serenely. 'You may not. You have a wife now, and a daughter. I have a husband, and daughters. We are more mature, and must forget that which is past. But I would like us to be friends.'

He snorted. 'Friends! Pen, it is not as a

friend that I think of you! I long for you with every atom of my body and soul. Dear God, I've done my best to forget; I lie in bed with Frances and make love to her and try to mean the words I whisper. But it is for you that my true love lies dormant in my breast. For you that I burn!'

She said sadly, 'We gave promises, Philip, which we cannot deny. You to your wife, I to myself. I don't count the promises made to Rich when we wed. *Those* promises died with my first child. Now we have an agreement, which is quite different. We have agreed that I shall have my own friends and lead my own life, to a certain extent. But I shall look after my children and our home. I've seen, remember, what happens to a family when the wife is unfaithful. Now that I'm a woman grown I know why mother behaved the way she did, and love her better because I understand her more. But I could not subject my children to such a life. They must come first with me.'

'Then it is finished, between us? Over, because I have a wife and you've born daughters?'

She nodded dumbly, moved close to tears by the despair in his voice.

He seemed to collect himself. 'Very well,' he said harshly. 'May I accompany you to your mother's parlour? It seems she wants her daughters with her, this evening.'

But when they drew level with her own room she stopped him.

'I am tired, it has been a long day,' she said. 'I shall retire to bed now. Will you tell my mother?'

He nodded, and left her.

Penelope prepared for bed, helped Lavender choose her gown and petticoats for the morning, then saw the maid make up the fire and draw the curtains round her bed before she let herself quietly out of the room.

Much later, she heard the door open softly and heard the soft pad of stockinged feet as someone crossed the room. She sat up in bed and drew the curtains back with an alarming swish.

Philip stood there in the firelight, his face looking guilty and vulnerable.

'Just let me be with you, talk to you,' he said. 'I can no more stop loving you than I can stop breathing!'

Penelope swung her legs out of bed and reached for her bed-gown. She slung it round her shoulders and gestured him to the chair close to the fire. When he was seated she sat down at his feet on a padded stool.

'What is there to say?' she asked listlessly. 'We have said it all, Philip.'

'Not quite. You admit we love each other? Then *why* should we not follow our love to its natural conclusion? Indeed, Frances would be the richer for your submission, because I will not then blame her for inadequacies she cannot help! The only true inadequacy is that she is not you. And will you rob your children to give me love? Of course not! You have love and to spare, for us all.'

He stood up as he spoke and pulled her to her feet. Holding her away from him by the elbows, he said seriously, 'Can you look into my eyes and believe me false? Can you deny that you love me?'

She looked into his eyes, and read only truth, and the depth of his pain. Without a word she went into his arms.

They were lovers once more. The wheel had turned full circle.

SEVEN

'We are both, in a sense, grass widows, so why don't you come down to Wanstead with me?' Lettice asked Penelope. 'Dotty has rushed off with her horrid husband to visit friends in York, of all places, and you've spent weeks at Leighs already this summer. But London is unhealthy at this time of year, and in any event, all the fun seems to have gone out of life with Leicester and Essex fighting in the Netherlands, and Sidney with them.'

'Yes, I'll come for a while,' Penelope agreed. Her heart bled for her mother in one way, for she knew that what made Lettice saddest was not her husband's absence, nor that of her favourite Devereux son. It was the death of the little imp, Robbie, the child of her old age.

Unfortunately, she also knew that Christopher Blount, the Leicesters' master of horse, would be more available at Wanstead than he was in London. And she knew that her mother was suffering under the fierce displeasure of the Queen.

It had been bad enough when Leicester had been made Governor of the United Provinces, against her specific commands, but when she heard that Lady Leicester planned to join him there, complete with a train which she, as a Queen might have envied, her fury knew no bounds.

'She would have clapped me in the Tower for two pins,' Lettice told her daughter, her eyes wide with the narrowness of her escape. 'I tell you, Penny, I could have wept! The thought of going over to a foreign country, and being almost a Queen, was so glorious. And then I should have been with my husband, which would have given us both such pleasure.' She sighed, then brightened. 'But since I can't go to the United Provinces, I will go to Wanstead. My friends will be glad to see me.'

'Are you *sure* you want me with you?' Penelope asked frankly. 'I do hate playing gooseberry, and Rich would be delighted to see me back at Leighs so soon.' She laughed. 'One thing we have in common, mother, is the ability to rouse the love and protective instincts of our husbands, whatever we may be up to!'

'Minx!' Lettice said reprovingly. 'I am not up to anything and nor can you be, with Philip on the continent. As for your not being welcome, you should know by now that the last thing I wish for is an unwilling or unwanted guest. Didn't you know? Leicester had need of his master of horse, so he is on his way across the channel, probably, at this very moment.'

She left Penelope shaking her head sadly. 'Shameless,' she muttered. 'Quite shameless. And she wonders why Dotty is such a hussy!'

★ ★ ★ ★

Autumn found her back at Leicester House with her mother, after spending a happy summer between Wanstead and Leighs. Her three adorable daughters were growing fast, and beautifully, and she even found Rich's company pleasanter than usual. She knew he had a mistress but the woman was discreet and never drew attention to herself in a way likely to bring Penelope embarrassment, and she also knew, without false pride, that Rich loved his wife far more deeply than he could ever have loved his changing array of mistresses. It was just that during her absences from home he needed the comfort which only a woman could give. And he needs other women to bolster his self-confidence, which I treat so harshly when I obviously prefer my own company to his, Penelope told herself.

She planned to return to Leighs for Christmas, and then go back to London again for the New Year celebrations.

'I have a gift from myself and Rich, and another from Essex, to give her Grace,' she told her mother. 'Which is a good excuse for joining in the revelry.'

But before Christmas came, she had a caller, and all thoughts of revelry went out of her head.

'Why, Lady Pembroke! Oh, Mary, it's good to see you!' Penelope cried, on answering a servant's summons to 'speak to the lady in the big parlour.'

Mary kissed her hostess, then said

quietly, 'Sit down, my dear. I have bad news.'

Penelope felt the colour drain from her face. She sat down, obedient as a child, and said in a small, faint voice, 'Is he dead?'

'No, but he has been dangerously wounded. He has a thigh wound. My younger brother Robert is with him, and writes to me regularly. At first he was hopeful and confident, but he seems less so. I felt I had to tell you.'

Penelope got to her feet like a sleep-walker. Swaying, she said 'Where is he?'

'He was injured at Zutphen, but he was moved from there to Arnhem. He is at the house of a woman named Gruitthueissens who is a famous nurse, apparently, and he has the best doctors.'

'I must go to him,' Penelope said slowly. 'I must go *now*. I will ring for my woman, and she will pack some things for me.'

Mary stood up and led Penelope back to her seat. 'My dear, you must not. Indeed, for his sake, you cannot. His wife is with him, helping the doctors. You must not think of going.'

'Frances is with him? But it will be *me* he wants.'

Mary took a deep breath. 'Penelope, you cannot know that. It is a year since you last saw him, and Frances has been with him most of the time. And in any event, if you go to him now you will bring into the open an affair which can only harm his reputation, and would undoubtedly ruin his marriage.'

'Then I will write, and ask him if I may go.'

'You poor child. Frances opens his letters for him now; he cannot do so for himself whilst he is so weak.' She hesitated. 'Penelope, perhaps I was wrong to tell you. But it is becoming common knowledge at court, and I was afraid you might hear it casually, and suffer terribly.'

'Yes, I'm sorry. You are right and I'm

glad I know. But dear God, not to be able to go to him! Not even to *write!*'

'You and Philip have been cautious and sensible over your love for each other,' Mary said. 'You have thought always of others, making sure that no-one was hurt by your feelings. Because of that, there are scarcely more than two or three people who know that you are lovers. Certainly Frances does not suspect for one moment that there is anything between you now but friendship. Even I did not know for certain until I saw your face when I told you of his wound. Your own brother Essex knows, perhaps, and your mother, and Leicester. But of all Philip's friends, and he has many, not one suspects that your friendship is more than that. Would you want to risk their respect for Philip? I am very sure you would not!'

'It's all right. I forgot everything for a moment but that he would want me near him,' Penelope said. 'I shan't try to write, nor go to him. But I beg you, Mary, let me know when you get news.'

'I will,' Mary promised.

★ ★ ★ ★

When news came, it was of his deterioration. Gangrene had set in, and against it they could wage no war.

He had greeted death with pleasure, they said, after three weeks of such agony. But Robert Sidney, who had adored Philip, cried like a child, telling the men about his brother's corpse that he would rather have died himself than see Philip suffer so.

And from the sorrow and suffering, Penelope crept away, to Leighs. She told no-one of her loss and few people realised that she and Philip had shared more than a friendship. She was pregnant again, and only the child, she thought, gave her the courage to go on. For this baby would be a boy. She knew it without the faintest shadow of a doubt, and though he was no child of Philip's she believed he would have something of Philip about him.

Leighs welcomed her with its peace and beauty, as it always had. Her one-time friend and ally, Catherine Rich, had left some years before to marry one of the Howards, but even with querulous Auntie Freda Rich helping to run the house, she was happy there.

I will find peace here, she told herself, and heal my hurts. Then I will try to be satisfied by what I have—my marriage and my children—and will not expect, again, to have such a bounty of love.

★ ★ ★ ★

'A son at last, Penny! God, he's an ugly lump, though. Did you suffer much, giving birth to him?'

Penelope turned on Essex crossly.

'You know *nothing* of babies, my lad is beautiful,' she told him. 'I know he's large now, but he's getting on! He's not a helpless little creature any more, in fact I think he's going to be the most intelligent of my children.'

'No doubt about *that*, since he's the only boy,' Essex said with the conceit of a male for male brains. 'He isn't any uglier than any other baby, but I had to say something to rouse you. I can't bear a woman who sits and sews and smiles at the fire whilst I'm talking to her. I should think you must drive Rich wild.'

'I do. But not with boredom,' Penelope said tartly, and was rewarded by his snort of mirth. 'Get to the point, brother dear! Whenever you come a-visiting at Leighs it is because you want something. What this time?'

'Nothing!' Essex said indignantly. 'I thought I ought to see this lad of yours, have a word with Rich, perhaps, get a breath of country air ...'

His voice trailed away and Penelope thought that whatever he wanted, he was unwilling to reveal it yet.

'How is the Queen?' she said, changing

the subject. 'Has she forgiven you for being your mother's son and Dotty's brother?'

'The Queen would forgive me anything,' Essex said complacently. 'Women do, you know. Elizabeth was very strange to most people after the Queen of Scots lost her head, but she kept *me* close. Not that I had anything to do with beheading Mary Stuart,' he added.

Penelope laughed. 'Essex, you're crazy,' she declared. 'I could have sworn it was you under that hood.'

Her brother grinned. 'Don't take everything so literally, sister,' he advised. 'Mind you, I did write to the King of Scots. I asked him to intervene to save Davison, the secretary who took stick from Elizabeth for the beheading, though it was about as much to do with that poor devil as it was with me.'

'You asked King James ...! Essex, sometimes I think you really *are* crazy,' gasped Penelope. 'You asked James to intervene to save the man whom the Queen is officially blaming for the beheading of James's own mother! Or is it I who am crazy? Did I just *imagine* you said you'd written to James?'

'Oh, I see what you mean,' Essex said after a frowning pause. He grinned at her. 'Courage, sister. I was always impetuous. I must say I'd not thought of it in that light, but now you mention it, perhaps it wasn't very tactful. James never answered my letter, anyway, so no harm done.'

'And what else is happening at court? Will you go from here to Whitehall, or wherever the court is at present?'

'We go on a progress,' Essex said proudly. 'It includes North Hall. And that brings me to my reason for seeking you here, Penny. Why don't you come along? I know you're happy enough in the country now that ...' he paused, tact for once making itself felt so that he hesitated to use Philip's name. 'Well, anyway, the Warwicks have always been kindness itself to us, and Aunt Ann would love you to come. And I'm always happy to be in the company of my pretty sister,' he added disingenuously.

'Well, I don't know,' Penelope temporised, sorely tempted. It seemed such an age since she had been at court, with young men writing sonnets to her fine eyes and others dancing with her half the night. And she was very fond of Aunt Ann and the Earl of Warwick.

'You will be escorted to North Hall, and then I must go to Greenwich to be with Elizabeth,' Essex said. 'Come on, Pen! Leicester has gone back to the Netherlands so the Queen needs me and I can't see as much of you as I'd like. Besides, I've got no money, and the Queen is the only person who can remedy that defect! I wish I'd been on Drake's expedition when he captured the *San Philipe* with all her treasure on board. A share in that would have financed another army, and I could have returned to the Netherlands with Leicester.'

'What about Drake attacking the shipping in Cadiz harbour, and stopping the Spanish invasion plans? Would you have enjoyed that part of the venture?'

'Most of all,' breathed Essex. 'I want to be a soldier or a commander, Pen! The court is all very well, but there is not the excitement and companionship which one finds when soldiering. By the way, did I tell you the Queen has granted me the position of Master of Horse? It may not be much, but it is a very good beginning.'

'You did mention it,' admitted Penelope. 'You wrote me twice, you visited me whilst I was staying with Lady Pembroke and told me again. You pointed out the advantages of such a post over dinner last night, and you did mention this morning at breakfast, that in your new position as Master of the Queen's horses ...'

'I thought I had,' nodded Essex and Penelope reflected, not for the first time, that sarcasm was absolutely wasted on him.

'I will come to North Hall,' she decided. 'Can you escort me in a couple of day's time? I must make all tidy here before I leave.'

'Ah,' said Essex, looking guilty. 'Well Penny, I think Anthony Bagot had better escort you, instead of me. I don't like to be away from the Queen for too long—you never know who might shoulder into her confidence. So if you don't mind ...'

'Anthony would be a delightful companion,' Penelope said at once. 'We have known each other for so long, your esquire and myself. I daresay he can remember me when I was just a scrubby child in the schoolroom.'

'No, surely not?' Robert said with his customary frankness. 'For you are four years older than I, and quite six older than Tony.'

'Essex, you said earlier that Philip Sidney had left you his sword, and that you hoped to attain his place in the hearts of men,' Penelope said. 'If you wish to be held in esteem by women as well, have the goodness never to remind me of my age again! To be reminded that you are four years younger than me is bad enough, but saying Tony Bagot could not remember me as a girl is too much. Mend your manners or I'll not go to North Hall and you shall not come again to Leighs!'

Robert gazed at her for a moment, then gave one of his rare laughs. 'You're joking,' he said with certainty. 'But what does age matter, Penny, when a woman is as beautiful as you? I swear that in all my petticoat dealings I've not yet met a woman who could hold a candle to you. You are a great deal prettier than Dotty, and have twice as many brains.'

'For those kind words I will pack my baggage without further argument, and accompany Tony to North Hall at once,' Penelope said. 'I must tell my husband first, of course.'

'You tell him, I notice, you do not ask him.'

'Very quick of you. But I tell him nicely, you must understand!'

* * * *

Penelope was a welcome visitor. The Warwicks were childless, and had given the young Devereux plenty of affection, welcoming them to their homes as though they were in truth nephews and nieces, instead of merely being Leicester's step-children.

So now, Penelope settled down in the familiar room where she had been a guest, off and on, for over ten years. Because of the Queen's visit, she would be asked to share it with four or five of Elizabeth's gentlewomen, once the court was in residence.

She was staring out over the familiar park, when Lady Warwick entered the room after a soft tap on the door.

'Are you comfortable, Penny dear?'

'Yes thank you, Aunt Ann. I am most

grateful for your invitation, because I've been about so little in the past few months. It must be more than a year since I saw the Queen, for instance. What do you think I should wear for her reception?'

'What multitude of gowns,' Lady Warwick exclaimed, gazing at the garments which Lavender was hanging around the room. 'Whatever one may say about Rich, he certainly spoils you! You are the prettiest creature anyway, but in that froth of a gown you look like something out of a dream. Wear what you like, love, for you would glorify rags!'

'You are the best and kindest of women, Aunt Ann,' Penelope said earnestly. 'When I was young I used to wish ... but never mind that, only you are a born mother and your talents are not wasted, for you mother us all. Even the Queen who doesn't like women very much, loves her dearest Ann! Now be serious, though. What *shall* I wear tomorrow night?'

Lady Warwick considered. 'I shall be

wearing a very suitable dove-grey,' she remarked. 'The Queen will, of course, be clad in something glorious. If you can forgive me for a suggestion which so few young women would appreciate, my love, I would wear the least noticeable gown you possess. It is not that the Queen would be jealous, of course, but you know your mother has offended her deeply because she tries to out-dress her, if there is such an expression. I'd not wish her to vent her annoyance on you as well.'

'Choose something demure then, if you can see a gown which fits that description,' Penelope said, smiling.

'How about this leaf-brown taffeta, dear? It would do admirably, I'm sure.'

'I look very striking in that gown,' Penelope objected. 'Are you sure her Grace would not prefer something even plainer, like sackcloth and ashes?'

Lady Warwick laughed. 'Maybe she would,' she admitted. 'And that reminds me, I *must* be firm with Dotty this time.

She has brought a number of really tasteless gowns with her, all brightly coloured and low-cut. I shall have to try to ensure that she wears the least offensive of them, rather than the most.'

'But Dotty isn't here!' Penelope said.

'Well, but she is, dear. Not here at this minute, I admit, but that is because she has gone over to see an old friend of Tom Perrot's, who lives nearby. She will be back in time to dine with us.'

'Does the Queen know she's staying in the house?' Penelope asked incredulously. 'You know how she feels about Dotty, Aunt Ann! She's never forgiven the poor girl for that foolish whim of Leicester's to marry her to James of Scotland. Nor for her elopement, for that matter. You know how the Queen hates anything underhand, and that business was very underhand indeed. Mother and the Earl had all but signed a marriage treaty with someone else, you know, when Dotty ran off with Tom. And for all her sighs of love, she and Tom fight like dog and cat now, and are always applying to the Earl for money. They're as feckless as each other.'

'Yes, dear, I know,' Lady Warwick said placidly. 'But I've known Elizabeth since we were both girls, and I'm not afraid of her, whoever else may be. North Hall is my home, and I can invite whom I please to stay with me here. I think it is time that Elizabeth gave up this vendetta against Letty's children, for that's what it amounts to, you know. Perhaps she can't forgive Letty, but she's pleased enough to make a favourite of the boy. She should meet Dotty again, and see for herself that the girl's not all bad.'

'Well, if you think it wise,' Penelope said doubtfully. She had guessed from Essex's worries over leaving the Queen that his hold on her affections was not as secure as he could wish and she could imagine all too well how thoroughly it might be shaken by the Queen attacking Dotty in his very presence.

But how to mend matters? After much thought she decided that she would ask Lady Warwick to send a messenger to Essex. She would merely advise him of their sister's presence and he would then be able to decide what best to do.

Satisfied that she had arrived at the only possible solution, Penelope put the finishing touches to her appearance and went down to dinner.

★ ★ ★ ★

'Is that yellow silk gown truly the most suitable garment you could find to meet the Queen in? Dotty, it is by far the brightest colour here! Couldn't you just for once, be content to hide your light under a bushel?'

Dotty glanced contemptuously at her sister. 'No I could *not*,' she said roundly. 'Why should I? The old devil hasn't received me for five years, so she might as well see me properly. Besides, I *like* yellow! I had thought of wearing the poppy taffeta, but Aunt Ann said it was gaudy.'

'And does she approve of the yellow?'

Dorothy shrugged sulkily. 'Other people like it,' she said. Then, 'Why aren't we waiting with the Earl and Countess, in the driveway? Why are we stuck in here?'

'The sun is very warm, and there is a breeze,' countered Penelope. 'Do you want to freckle, and have your hair blown out of curl? It is more comfortable here.'

'Yes, but ...' began Dorothy, then she ran to the window. 'They're here, Penny! Ooh, how handsome our brother looks in brown velvet—but he must be sweltering! The Queen looks very elegant, her gown is beech green.' She turned away from the window for a moment. 'Isn't it odd, Penny, that the Queen, who is old, can still look young and charming? Close to, you can see the paint and the lines, but from here she looks—not beautiful exactly, but most attractive.'

'She has presence,' said Penelope wisely.

'And that is only a beginning. She wears clothes elegantly so that she makes simple gowns look special. Prepare to curtsy dear! I think they're coming indoors.'

But it was only the Earl of Warwick, good Uncle Ambrose, hurrying into the room with his thin white hair on end and his face creased with worry.

'Dorothy, my dear, the Queen is angry that you are here. I'm afraid you must keep to your room until she leaves. She will not listen to Lady Warwick, not yet at any rate. Ann says she will bring her round, but for the time being you had better go to your room, and later she will talk to the Queen and make her see reason.'

To Penelope's surprise, Dorothy seemed resigned rather than annoyed, as though she had expected something of the sort.

'I'll go up then, Uncle Ambrose,' she said. 'But *do* remind Aunt Ann to speak to the Queen!' She turned to Penelope. 'And *please* see that the servants don't forget me. There is some marvellous food, all my favourite things, so make sure I'm sent a well-filled tray. I love those little lobster patties, oh, and the crayfish which aunt's cook does in that marvellous sauce.'

'I'll see to it,' Penelope said, unable to repress a smile at her sister's unashamed interest in her dinner. 'And now run upstairs, Dotty. No sense in offending the Queen before a word has been said on your behalf.'

Dorothy ran up the stairs and was lost to view in a flurry of daffodil silk; but the worst was yet to come. As soon as Penelope set eyes on Essex's face she saw the rigidly contained fury which he was scarcely troubling to hide. The Queen was coolly polite to Penelope, but she could see that Elizabeth itched to give Essex a good dressing down for his sulky and childlike fury, and could scarcely blame her.

Light refreshments were eaten, and then the Queen was escorted by Aunt Ann up to the room she would occupy during her stay. To Penelope's distress, no sooner had

Lady Warwick reappeared than Essex took himself off upstairs, his long legs devouring the flight two at a time.

'I've not seen him in such a paddy since he was eight or nine,' Penelope told her aunt, as they prepared a tray for Dorothy. 'Then, his temper was understandable perhaps, because he got his own way with mother almost always, and if for some reason she was firm, then a display of sulks or furious temper soon brought her back under Essex's thumb. But the Queen—well, that's a different kettle of fish!'

'He's doing Dotty's cause no good at all,' Lady Warwick said distractedly. 'Oh, the foolish boy! No-one will be able to reason with Elizabeth after this.'

'Then Dotty had better get used to having meals on a tray,' Penelope said practically. She eyed the tray critically. 'But that is a perfectly delicious meal, and nicely presented, though I say it as shouldn't. I'll take it up to her myself,

Aunt Ann, to save the servants. They are so busy.'

As she drew nearer to the door which led to the Queen's room however, she found her footsteps getting slower and slower. What a tremendous amount of noise they were making, those two highly coloured, high-spirited people! She could hear the Queen's carefully controlled voice, sounding increasingly annoyed, and then Robert. But he was shouting at Elizabeth, as though she were a mere woman who had annoyed him, and not his Queen. She heard his hot and heedless threats rise to a crescendo, and then the door burst open and he shot into the corridor, almost upsetting her tray with the speed of his passing.

'Essex!' Penelope cried. 'Stop this minute and tell me what you've done.'

His face was frightening, a brick-red colour, and the fury on it would have made his mother give him his way at once, for fear he might have a seizure.

He did not reply to her question but caught her arm and hurried her along the corridor with him, heedless of the ripping of the delicate lace on her sleeve.

They reached the door behind which Dorothy had lurked all evening, and Essex burst inside without knocking.

Dorothy, bored, had put herself to bed. At their abrupt entrance she squeaked and jumped, scattering sweetmeats from the bowl in front of her onto the counterpane.

'What do you want?' she said rudely, glaring at her brother. 'I'll thank you not to burst into my room like that, Essex, and for goodness sake let go of Penelope's sleeve! You've torn her lace, and you'll make her drop my tray I shouldn't wonder. I've waited long enough, but it looks good. Pass it over, Penny.'

Essex said tersely, 'Get up!' and tore back the bedclothes, bringing another squeak from Dorothy, so abruptly revealed. 'You must leave at once, Dotty, since your presence offends the Queen so much. I shall leave as well, rather than see my family so dishonoured. Get *up*, I said!'

'Now? It must be midnight,' Dorothy exclaimed, showing a distressing tendency to curl down beneath the covers once more and ignore her brother's passionate instructions. 'Just go away, Essex, and let me eat my supper in peace. Penny, make him go away. He's always had a fancy for getting his own way, but ...'

'Get UP!' roared Essex and Dorothy began to cry, getting uncertainly out of bed, standing in her crushed white petticoat with her curls dishevelled, looking more like a frightened little girl than the naughty and sophisticated Lady Perrot.

Penelope laid the tray down on the bed and put her arm round her sister. 'She's shivering,' she announced. 'Get out of here, Essex, and I'll help her dress. We'll be down as soon as she's warmly clad. And when we come downstairs we'll discuss things rationally with the Warwicks.'

Essex departed, grumbling, but as soon

as they appeared downstairs, he sent a servant to pack Dorothy's belongings.

'I shall take you to our mother, at Kenilworth,' he said sulkily, when Dorothy sobbed that she had nowhere to go. 'And then I'm off, I can tell you! No more hanging round whilst that woman prefers a Devonshire clod to the noblest blood in England. I shall join Uncle Leicester in the Netherlands and if I die in the war, why should I care? Better an honourable death than dishonour here!'

'I take it you are blaming Ralegh for *something*,' Penelope said sweetly. 'Though what it can be I confess I cannot imagine. And why should you receive dishonour in England? You foolish boy, it is Dotty who should be angry and you can see for yourself she is not! Now calm yourself, do.'

But nothing would calm him. Not Lady Warwick's quiet kindness nor the Earl's brisk commonsense. Dorothy had been publicly slighted by the Queen; Elizabeth had said unforgivable things about Essex's mother. In short, he took the slight personally, and when denied his own way, was determined to extract revenge. He did not say in so many words that the Queen must suffer for her opinion, but no-one had the slightest illusion that he did not mean that. She enjoyed his company and required his presence; very well, he would deprive her of both! He had long been jealous of Ralegh and had done his best to set the Queen against the older man, but without success. Very well, then let Ralegh have her!

The fact that he was, in fact, cutting off his nose to spite his face did not occur to him, but Penelope knew it was true. Away from the excitement of the court he would sulk and grow weary soon enough, and without the Queen's constant company he would worry terribly that some other courtier would take his place.

But his vanity had been wounded, and

he must hurt back, even though it cost him dear.

'I shall leave too, and since the very name of Devereux will probably cause the Queen to have an apoplexy shortly, perhaps it is for the best,' Penelope said resignedly. 'I'll go with Dotty to Kenilworth.'

Lady Warwick protested; she had looked forward to Penelope's visit, and did not wish to be deprived of the treat. But a quiet word from her favourite niece soon made her withdraw her objections.

'I dare not let Essex escort the poor child whilst he is in such an evil humour,' Penelope told Lady Warwick. 'I'm sure he would not hurt Dotty deliberately, but he might easily pick a quarrel with someone else and just go off and leave her to make her own way to Kenilworth. And I believe I was right in a way about the Queen; she isn't going to forgive this night's work easily. It will be better for everyone if there is no reminder of Dotty, or of Essex, for that matter.'

'She'll probably forgive Essex sooner than I shall,' Lady Warwick said a trifle grimly. 'How *could* he make such a scene in my house, Penny? If *only* I'd been allowed to approach the Queen on the subject of Dotty in my own time ... But there, what's done cannot be undone. Take care of Dotty, and come and see us again soon.'

'I will,' promised Penelope. 'And how glad I am that I chose the brown silk, for it will do very well to travel in. Perhaps you would send Lavender on with my baggage tomorrow?'

★ ★ ★ ★

Instead of riding for Kenilworth, however, Essex escorted his sisters to Leicester House, because he wanted to ride for Gravesend the following morning to get aboard a boat for the Netherlands.

Next morning, therefore, Penelope got up early, leaving Dorothy still fast asleep, and went downstairs to bid her brother goodbye.

He was eating a huge breakfast, morosely shovelling food into his mouth whilst he read a book, propped up before him against a manchet of bread.

He jumped when Penelope spoke, and knocked over his book.

'Don't creep about, Penny,' he said crossly. 'Come to see me off, have you? By tomorrow I shall be on the continent. There may not be much glory won in their battles, but at least I shall have action.'

He finished the food on his plate, took a swig of ale, and stood up.

'Goodbye, Penny; sorry your treat turned out so badly. But you needn't have left, you know. Dotty would have been quite safe with me.'

'Oh, yes?' Penelope said dryly. 'Alone here, with my mother's servants, to ride to her home alone, or to ride to Kenilworth? It would be unworthy of Sidney, I believe.'

Essex had the grace to look slightly

ashamed of himself. 'I didn't think,' he mumbled. 'Will you take Dotty to Kenilworth for me, Penny? I *cannot* wait in England, or she will think leaving North Hall just an empty gesture.'

'She? You'd better say the Queen, brother,' advised Penelope. 'Of course I'll go with Dotty, but have you no friend who might escort us? It is a long way for two women to ride alone, with only servants.'

'Hang it, the court are with the Queen at North Hall, or in their country homes, and everyone else is in the Netherlands with Leicester,' grumbled Essex, looking harried. 'Oh, but I've got it! Blount's elder brother—not the eldest, the middle one—he might do it. He's a lawyer, at Gray's Inn, but he's done a bit of soldiering and he's at court now and then. I'll send a servant round to his lodgings to ask.'

'How close a friend is he?' Penelope asked cautiously. 'I don't remember meeting him before.'

'Well, we fought a duel once,' Essex

161

said, grinning. 'But damn it, he's Chris's brother and Chris and I are thick enough. I daresay he'll do it to oblige me.'

★ ★ ★ ★

'I was sorry to hear that your visit to the Countess of Warwick had been cut short; but I daresay you'll return when this annoying business has been forgotten,' Charles Blount said politely as he and the sisters rode out of London the next morning.

Penelope made a non-committal reply and sniffed the air with appreciation. How stuffy and smelly London was in the summer, and how good it was to be riding a lively mare, in the company of an intelligent young man, back into the country!

Glancing at Blount whenever his attention was elsewhere, she saw a well set up young man of about her own age, whose thick, dark brown hair grew into a widow's peak on his high forehead. He had very dark eyes, as dark as her own, and when he glanced across at her and grinned, his eyes seemed to reflect the sympathy and humour, as well as a degree of wry patience.

And he needed all those attributes during the ride. Dotty's behaviour would have tried the patience of a saint, Penelope thought. First, she wanted to ride fast while they were still in town streets, then she dropped behind, dawdling and pulling in her mount to peer down into gardens or over hedges. Then she wanted a drink and some food barely an hour after breakfast. Finally, she began to tell them stories about her marriage with Tom Perrot which made Blount's hair stand on end—or should have, thought Penelope. She noticed several times that an alarmed expression crossed his face, as he wondered what Lady Perrot would say next, and then she hastily threw herself into the breach, laughing at Dorothy's more extravagant statements, persuading her sister and Blount to laugh with her.

When they arrived at Kenilworth, Lettice insisted that Blount should stay for a couple of days before undertaking the journey back to his lodgings.

'Your brother has been wounded, as you know, but is mending fast,' she said in the direct and friendly way which made young men adore her. 'I shall receive letters from my husband in a day or so, and he always mentions Chris—he thinks so highly of him. If you care to stay you shall read of their doings yourself.'

He stayed for a couple of days, and the time passed pleasantly enough. Dorothy tried to flirt with him, but rather to Penelope's surprise, he made it politely evident that he had no time for flirting.

'A young man so serious would never do for *me*,' Dorothy said that night as she and Penelope prepared for bed.

'Nor for me,' Penelope agreed. 'But then we wouldn't do for him, for we are both married. You'll have to try your tricks on someone more light-minded, young woman.'

'Oh, there are plenty of interested young men about,' Dorothy said. She glanced curiously at her sister. 'I'm surprised that you've not done some exploring yourself, to liven the monotony of living with Rich.'

'I surprise myself, sometimes,' Penelope admitted. 'But I'd not find a man to equal Philip, no, not even half as good. And until I do, it might as well be Rich as anyone else.'

'How strange you are!' Dorothy said frankly. 'But there, we're not at all alike. What do you think of mother's horsemaster?'

'Chris Blount? Very good looking and as nasty as can be; perhaps it's as well that the older brother doesn't admire yellow-heads. Go away now, Dotty, I'm tired. I'll see you in the morning.'

EIGHT

Penelope sat dreaming in her room at Wanstead, enjoying the freshness of evening which had come with the twilight, following a hot and breathless summer day. It was her first trip away from Leighs for a while, and she thought guiltily that she was enjoying, as much as anything, the freedom from her children's constant company.

Over the years, to be with her witty, amoral mother had become an almost unalloyed pleasure. The spiteful comments which Lettice had seemed to find it impossible to repress when in the company of her eldest daughter had begun to lessen when they failed to bring a satisfactory response, and in their new-found amity, mother and daughter drew closer still because of the love and loyalty they both felt for Essex.

But now, Penelope's mind was going back over the years since Philip had died. So many years had slipped away, their passing almost unnoticed. She had known she would never find anyone to replace him in her affections; he was unique. But she had believed that somewhere, was a man who could fill the emptiness in her heart in a different, but equally satisfactory, way.

Then she had met the man.

She lay back in her chair, considering. He was a second son, and had duelled with Essex once and quarrelled furiously with him many times. He was a dandy, and something of a hypochondriac over his health. He was witty, but not the wittiest, a leader of men but not the foremost; handsome but not the handsomest. Yet to conjure up his image before her mind's eye gave her the keenest delight. She did so now, seeing the strong-growing tufty black hair, the bright, dark eyes, the square chin which he strove to make fashionably sensitive by wearing a small, pointed beard.

But this paragon, she reminded herself, does not want me. Not that she had ever offered herself, but she had been unable to resist his friendship. Yet he kept carefully clear of her, would not dream of partnering her for more than one dance, or of walking with her other than along the most frequented by-ways.

So many others were finding love, why could not she do the same? There was Frances Sidney, who had married Essex and borne him children. Essex treated her abominably, of course, and was still seducing any maid of honour who glanced at him twice, but Frances loved her husband, hurt and infuriated by him though she must often have been.

And then cousin Vernon. She smiled at the thought of her favourite relative. Elizabeth Vernon was her quiet little

168

country cousin who had come up to court to be one of the Queen's women, and had fallen in love with and won the heart of Henry Wriothesley, Earl of Southampton. Since the Queen frowned on the marriage, they were enjoying all the thrills of a forbidden love affair, spiced with secret meetings, dewed with unhappy tears of parting.

My own mother, Penelope thought, has more love in her life than I! When the Earl of Leicester had died some years earlier, she had promptly married Chris Blount. It had caused talk, of course. Some uncharitable folk had said Lettice must have poisoned the Earl to win her horsemaster, but most agreed that the strain of commanding the land forces at the time of the Armada had been too much for a heart already overstrained by corpulence and sudden bouts of furious activity, alternating with slothfulness.

Why does the man I want to want me not pursue me? she wondered. Sometimes she thought she saw cool speculation bordering on dislike in his eyes, but the expression was fleeting, and soon replaced by his usual friendliness.

Outside the window the night breeze sighed, a sleepy bird twittered, moonlight spilled silver onto the lawn. Inside, the house settled down, creaking, to its night-time repose. Somewhere in the house, Lettice and Chris would be climbing into bed. Mother, Penelope calculated, is fifty and Chris something like thirty. Scarcely more than half her age, yet it is easy to see he still finds her fascinating. Why is it that I could have any man at my feet but the man I want, and I am young still, and not bad-looking.

Sleep was not going to come tonight. Of late, she had been suffering from sleepless nights, and hated them, and she knew that part of the fault lay in the warmth of the bed and the stuffiness of the room, for she would not have dreamed of going to sleep with the window open.

She was seized by a desire to roam the moonlit gardens. It would be easy enough, she could slip downstairs, out of a side-door, and roam in the sweet coolness of the grounds until she began to feel drowsy. The thought appealed to her, but the idea of meeting her young stepfather did not. He had shown only the greatest discretion in his dealings with her, but she had occasionally felt his glance resting upon her in a speculative, greedy way which she disliked. She pondered the possibility of his also being smitten by a desire for night-wandering, but dismissed it. Lettice, with a houseful of pretty servants, would not take kindly to her young husband's absence from the marital bed on an excuse so indefinite as a walk around the grounds. No, her mother would see that Chris did not stray from her bed, where he belonged.

She stood up and slipped into a flimsy robe. Her soft leather slippers, with their scuffed toes and flattened heels, would be ideal for making her silent way through the house. She wondered whether to tie a handkerchief over her loose hair, but decided against it. How foolish to guard against the gentle breeze, when she *wanted* to feel its fingers lifting the heavy mass of her golden hair, and stroking her overheated skin.

As she had anticipated the house was wrapped in slumber, not a servant, not even a dog, stirring as she trod soundlessly down the stairs and along the hall to the side door which she had decided to use. The bolts were heavy, but slid back soundlessly, though the door itself creaked on a low, grumbling note as she pushed it open. Smiling at her own fluttering heartbeats, she stepped onto the paving and closed the door behind her.

Now that she was outside, she could taste the sweetness of a nearby cedar tree, and see how the grass was wet with dew. She strolled forward, enjoying this new aspect of the familiar. She glanced back at the house, hoping that no watcher would spy on her from behind those bright, soulless windows and think her a night-wanderer, up to no good.

She did not cross the lawn because of the windows; instead, she walked stealthily into the shadow of some ornamental trees which formed a pleached avenue leading to the wild garden. There was a pool there, with fish in it, and a little stream. And beside the stream, a rustic hut, with cane chairs and cushions. She would make her way there and sit down for a while, perhaps even doze, whilst the stream sang its song and the night air cooled her.

But before she had taken more than a few paces out of the end of the avenue, she glanced back. Something had brought her head round with a jerk—the snap of a twig, a limb brushing past a summer-laden shrub? She hesitated, then walked forward again. It was only a shadow—but she could have sworn it had moved!

Abruptly, the night became full of sounds

she had not noticed before; menacing sounds. She glanced back again—there *was* something, or someone—behind her. She began to move more quickly and heard the movements behind her become more definite. Whoever it was had broken into a run.

It is probably one of the servants—or Chris—or my mother, Penelope thought, but the thought did not convince. Suddenly the darkness and the moonlight could only harbour evil; she wanted to run back to the house, but he—she—*it*—was between her and the familiar bulk of Wanstead. She told herself to turn and face her pursuer, but instead her heart gave a leap and she was running, running desperately through the silver and black shadowed orchard, ducking under low boughs, dodging around silvery trunks, trying desperately to escape whatever followed.

She burst into the wild garden, glancing back once more, seeing that her pursuer was no werewolf or faery but a tall, active man. Commonsense told her he could outrun her, would presently fall upon her and bear her to the ground, that she should not run further from the house and safety, but she cared not a straw for commonsense. She was all impulse, the impulse to escape. She knew, as she dodged desperately across the wild garden, what the deer feels like when it hears the hounds or how the hare feels when it sees the coursers.

Desperately, she flung herself down in the long grass behind some bushes, then wriggled forward until she felt safer. She could hear her pursuer's shoes thudding on the turf of the orchard, then he was level with her hiding place, slowing down, uncertain. She felt her heartbeats, hammering in her ears, would give her away, then saw his attention caught by the chattering stream.

Something about the turn of his head was achingly familiar, and before she fully realised what she was doing she had moved sharply, saying 'Philip?'

As soon as the word was uttered she knew that if it had been Philip's shade, it had been behaving in a very unghostlike fashion. She cowered down against the ground again.

The man turned, and dived into the bushes. She shrieked, her terror suddenly only half-real, for even as he moved she recognised him. It was Charles Blount.

'What on *earth* are you doing, running through the garden in your night-robe?'

Careless of dignity, Penelope clutched his arm, her eyes still wide with recent panic. 'Good God, how you frightened me,' she said. 'I thought you were a ghost or a robber, or worse!'

He did not push her away, but made no attempt to hold her in comfort.

'Have I interrupted an assignation?' he asked coldly. 'I imagine you were expecting my brother? No doubt he was earlier than you anticipated and is already awaiting you in the summer house.'

'Waiting for me? Your brother?' Penelope said, mystified. 'No, indeed! I fancy your brother and my mother have been in bed for several hours.' The significance of his remark suddenly struck her and she stiffened. 'Are you accusing me of having an affair with your brother Chris?' she said haughtily. '*Can* that be what you mean?'

'*Can* it be that you expect me to believe Chris shares a roof with you and does not share your bed?' Charles said, mimicking her outraged tone. 'I know my brother, and at first I could not understand the complacency with which he treated your mother's possessiveness. Then I remembered there had been rumours about you and Philip Sidney, and that it was commonly known you'd taken no lover since his death. What is that, six years? And then I *knew.*'

'It is longer than that,' Penelope said, her voice suddenly desolate. 'And I have no lover, least of all your brother, whom I heartily detest. It may surprise you to

177

know that he finds my mother perfectly adequate. And now I shall return to my room. I left it to find some coolness, after the heat of the day. Goodnight to you.'

His hand shot out and caught her wrist. 'No you don't,' he said coolly. 'If I am wrong, I must apologise. But let us first make sure that I *am* wrong. Come with me to the summer house, for I'll wager we'll find brother Chris cooling his heels there!'

She swung round and marched ahead of him, her back stiff as a ramrod, her mind seething with speculation. Could this be why he had never shown more than a reluctant friendliness towards her? A mistaken belief that she was Chris's mistress would make his behaviour perfectly understandable!

They reached the summer house and found it empty, as she had known it would be. Charles stepped inside, pulling her after him. 'No, he's not here yet; we will wait a little.'

'I'm going back to bed,' Penelope said, striving to make her voice firm. She suddenly found herself a little afraid of Charles. If he had shown more interest in her in the past, been friendlier! But she suddenly realised that she hardly knew him, that she was a long way from her room and the bell which would bring Lavender running.

'I'm sorry if I've wronged you,' he said in a gentler voice, 'And I am willing to admit that I have, for I can see from your face that you have been no lie-beside for my brother. Please don't run away, or I shall be forced to run after you, and that is far too energetic, twice in one evening. Come and talk to me! Now that I have banished my stupid suspicions, I want to know you better.'

There, in the moonlit garden house, they settled themselves on two creaking cane chairs, and opened their hearts to one another. Very soon they were chatting with the ease and intimacy of old and trusted friends, and Penelope was asking Charles what had brought him to Wanstead at such an hour.

'My elder brother, William, has died,' he said quietly. 'He has been ill for many months and we knew it was only a matter of time, but I thought I should inform Chris.'

'I'm sorry,' Penelope said. 'Will it affect Chris, though? He is very comfortably situated financially.'

'It won't affect *him,* but I am now Lord Mountjoy,' Charles said equably. 'You really do dislike my brother, don't you? I wish I'd realised it earlier!'

She smiled at him, still a little shy.

'Yes, it would have saved a lot of misunderstanding. But I think I should be returning to the house now, Charles. We must have been here for a couple of hours.'

'So we have, and talking of our brothers! In truth, there must be something lacking in me!'

'Perhaps something is lacking in us both, my lord.'

He looked at her sharply. 'Perhaps. But why so formal? You must continue to call me Charles, you know. I like to hear my name on your lips.'

He got to his feet and held out his hand to her. She took it and he pulled her to her feet and they stood for a moment breast to breast, looking searchingly into each other's eyes. Deliberately, she moved forward a little, so that their bodies touched. With the movement, a tingling message passed between them. Invitation and acceptance, Penelope thought and felt a surge of excitement which made her breath shorten.

'I would like to visit the summer house again,' he said, still with his eyes steady on hers. 'I shall be here for a few days yet. Would tomorrow night be a good time?'

'Tomorrow night,' she said. 'I think it might be a good time for visiting summer houses.'

They smiled at their own foolishness.

'This time, you shall be wooed in form,' he said, and patted her shoulder lightly. 'Now I will escort you back to the house, lest some other prowler, less well-intentioned than I, chances upon you.'

They walked back to the house and at the side door he said softly, 'You must go to your room now. I will wake a servant.'

She reached the foot of the stairs and looked back. He was standing by the door, watching her.

'This wooing, sir.'

'Yes, Pen?'

'I trust it will not be *too* protracted!'

She heard him laugh as she ran lightly up the flight.

★ ★ ★ ★

The meal was a good one, though the host had eaten sporadically; he had been too engrossed in arguing every point, occasionally applauding someone else's words, to bother much about his food. Essex, whatever his faults, was not a greedy man.

Leaning back in her chair, Penelope let her eyes run over the company. Next to her sat Charles, and their hands beneath the table were clasped together, for their love affair was a close-kept secret and must remain so. Southampton was sitting by Elizabeth, still unwed and yearning, and beside Vernon young Roger Manners, Earl of Rutland, cracked walnuts between his fingers and watched his host with bright devotion.

Chris Blount was there of course, and her mother. Sitting separately, it is true, but still very conscious of each other. Making up the party were Dorothy and her new husband, Henry Percy, Earl of Northumberland. She had married him within months of the riding accident which had killed ramshackle Tom Perrot, but already they bickered constantly, and now

Dorothy was sulking, sitting back in her chair and beating an impatient tattoo upon the tablecloth, because no-one was paying any attention to her.

Earlier, Lady Essex and Francis Bacon had been of the party, but poor Frances had felt ill—she was pregnant again and making heavy weather of it—and Francis Bacon, as Essex's secretary, had offered to escort her for a short walk to see if it would ease her queasiness. If not, she had said she would go straight to bed.

Penelope did not like Francis. She had been introduced to him as soon as she entered Essex House and knew of course that he was her brother's latest protegé. Though from what she had managed to gather, it was Essex who should have been grateful to Bacon, and not the other way round.

Francis, a tall, beautifully dressed young man with graceful movements and a face delicately painted, was, Essex assured her, positively brilliant. He had, with the help of his brother Anthony, built up a network of spies in Europe which rivalled any information source which Elizabeth had had at her disposal before.

'And he gives me advice, works for me in parliament, keeps my friends together,' enthused the Earl. 'He stuck his neck out for me in the commons, and ...'

'And very nearly got it severed,' interrupted Francis in a drawl. 'With your leave, sir, I shall never be so foolhardy again. It lost us more than it gained, unfortunately.'

'It lost you the Attorney-Generalship,' Essex admitted. 'And I'm sorry for it, as I was when Cecil made sure that Solicitor-General went elsewhere also. But I've made it up to you, haven't I?'

'You've been more than generous,' Francis said, and it was only afterwards that Penelope reflected his words had not, in fact, been an answer at all.

I don't trust him, she thought now, but

in this matter I must trust Essex; he knows the man.

The meal was ending at last. Chairs were being scraped back, nutshells thrown down onto the table. Penelope glanced at the clock. Another late night, and probably the men would talk for an hour or so yet.

She caught Charles' eye and they moved to the back of the room, their heads close.

'You are sleeping in your usual room?'

'Yes, my dear love; can you come to me?'

'I don't know, Pen. It is dangerous, under your brother's roof and with your mother watchful. But I will do my best. Can you let me in at the side door? I know it means you must stay awake until the men depart, but if you can do so, it will ease matters. I dare not try to remain behind; Bacon noticed last time, I'll swear it, though he didn't say a word.'

'I'll manage, somehow. After you leave, allow me thirty minutes for the rest of the house to go to bed, then come to the side door. I'll let you in.'

Without another word they parted, he to join the men, she the women. But as she sat and talked over the plans and ambitions of the Essex faction, as she knew the little group were being called, her mind returned constantly to Charles.

Love came to me late, she thought, but it has not found me more cautious. For Charles' sake, and for Essex's, she was circumspect, but she longed to blazon her love abroad, to announce it from the rooftops. She would always love Philip, and love his memory, as he had bidden his friends to do from his death-bed, but with her maturity she had known their relationship would never have had any permanence. He was beginning to love his wife and in time would have cleaved to her. Theirs had had all the romance and sweetness of a first, forbidden love. The relationship she shared with Charles was at once less romantic and yet deeper, so that she knew when the time came for her to choose between Rich, the children and her lover, there would *be* no choice. Charles already possessed her, body and soul.

Around her, the talk grew animated, and she joined in. It would not do to moon over Charles with her sharp-eyed mother present, and anyway, she would have him all to herself soon enough!

They discussed the theatre—had everyone seen *A comedy of errors?* It was unanimously declared excellent, and the new theatre, the Globe, was the pleasantest and most comfortable place to see a play. Someone mentioned the little Scottish Prince, Henry Stuart, and opinions were vouchsafed that he might well find himself King of England, one of these days.

But above all other topics, loomed the Queen and her court.

'Elizabeth was *furious* over that book, on the succession to the crown of England, which some damned Jesuit wrote, pretending it was the work of a Dutch

Protestant,' Lettice said with relish. 'I was furious, too, because it was patently a device to get my son blamed yet again for his closeness to the throne. But how I laughed when my niece told me of the Queen's fury! The book, you know, intimated that Essex might be Kingmaker, if not actual King!'

Frances had returned to the room, looking very pale, and now she spoke up with the acidity which Penelope thought sadly was the result of Essex's bad treatment of her.

'I think the whole business is ridiculous! Why should Essex want to be King? Absurd!'

'You wouldn't be Queen for a thousand pounds, would you, Fanny?' purred Dorothy. 'Why, you're never at court! Percy doesn't much care for London and wants me to live most of the time at Alnwick Castle—horrible, grim old pile—but I can tell you I wouldn't let him go to court without me!'

'You've no children yet, Dotty, but Frances and I have our young ones to keep us at home,' Penelope said quickly. She turned to Elizabeth Vernon. 'You are at court more than any of us, Vernon. Tell us how the Queen goes on.'

The talk continued, round and round the same old subjects, thought Penelope. She was actually beginning to nod when her mother got briskly to her feet, prodding her with the handle of her ivory fan.

'Penny! Don't you dare go off to sleep like an old woman! Southampton wants to walk his sweetheart back to Greenwich, or wherever she is staying, so we are breaking up the party early. There are candles on the table in the hall, so come and fetch yours. The cold air outside this room will soon wake you up!'

As they yawned their way up to bed, Penelope wondered whether she would ever be able to tell her mother about Charles. If she did, then she knew her secret would be safe enough, for because of her, Charles and Essex were friendly, and the Queen's wrath over the affair would effect them both.

But in the meantime, she would keep her own counsel.

NINE

'I feel so sick, Lavender. And so hot! Can you not open a window?'

'You're ill, milady. You sit there, right back from the fire, yet there is sweat on your face. And it is frosty outside. You ought to be in bed, not preparing the children's lessons.'

'I can't go to bed, with my sister Northumberland expected at any moment,' Penelope said, but her tone lacked conviction. 'Is it really frosty? I feel so hot.'

She stood up, meaning to walk over to the window and open it for herself, but to her surprise her knees buckled under her, as though they were made of jelly, and she slid slowly onto the sheepskin rug which Essex had given her as a New Year gift.

She heard Lavender run to her side with an alarmed cry, and then darkness enveloped her.

★ ★ ★ ★

Penelope opened her eyes. The pain thudding through her head increased with eye movement but she found if she was careful she could lift her lids and look straight before her.

It was dark in the room and for a moment she was puzzled, because she remembered falling onto her knees, pressed down by a curious weakness she could not control, and then it had been full day. She supposed vaguely that she was ill and that she must have slept. Or had she? The peace brought by sleep seemed to have been denied her for she was fiercely aware of a great heat beating in her body which was combining with long-drawn out aches in her limbs, pains in her joints, until they forced her back once more into uneasy wakefulness.

There was firelight, and flickering candle-light, she could tell by the shadows on the wall though she could see neither the glow from the hearth nor candleflame. She found she was afraid of the shadows, afraid even of this room, which did not seem like the familiar chamber where she had slept for so many years.

With infinite caution she moved her eyes, and saw a woman sitting by the bed, mending a child's gown. She tried to see who it was and the effort made her gasp as pain shot through her head, impaling her into frozen immobility.

The woman stood up and bent over her. Lavender's familiar face looked down on her, the mouth compressed with worry, the eyes tired.

'Why, you've woken up at last, milady,'

she said softly. 'Can you take a little nourishment? I've chicken broth ready to warm in a little pan, or some milk.'

Penelope became aware that she was thirsty. She said in a whisper, 'Milk,' and found that her voice croaked from disuse. She moved her hand on the counterpane until it was within her range of vision and saw it white and wasted.

Could this have happened in less than a *day?*

Lavender, neat and capable, was pouring the warm milk into a mug, testing the heat, then she set the pan down and came over to the bed.

'I must raise you a little, milady, to drink,' she said. 'Don't fret, I won't jolt you.'

But even the tiny movement of her arm easing beneath Penelope's head was painful so Penelope closed her eyes, determined not to show her discomfort.

'Drink now, milady.'

She opened her eyes, slowly, already

wanting to deny the milk, too tired by being lifted in the bed to want further exertion. But the mug was near, and the milk smelt good. She sipped twice, feeling the liquid smooth and bland on her tongue. Then she said 'Enough,' and Lavender lowered her back onto her pillows.

There were questions she should ask. Where was Dorothy? Was she going to be ill for long? Was it an infectious illness? But she asked none of them. The aching in her limbs was becoming intolerable and she was so hot! She groaned and felt with momentary pleasure the cool dampness of a cloth against her forehead. Then she somehow lost Lavender and the candlelit room, and was back in her world of fever and darkness, wandering alone through endless corridors of pain.

The next time she woke it was daylight, though she could not tell the time of day. The aching in her limbs seemed easier, and she fancied she was not as hot as she had been. She moved her head, opening her eyes and glancing across to the chair by the bed. Aunt Freda Rich was sitting there, her mousy little face anxious.

'Cousin, you are awake,' she said with relief. 'Lavender is resting. Is there anything I can get for you?'

'I'm thirsty, Aunt Freda. Might I have some water?'

'You had better have milk,' Freda said. 'Warm milk, dear. Lavender left some in a little pan and said to warm it if you woke.'

'Am I better?' Penelope asked lazily as Aunt Freda and one of the serving maids lifted her to lean against the pillows. 'Was it yesterday that I fell ill? I daresay my sister Northumberland has been seeing to the children for me.'

'Why, cousin, you've been ill more than three weeks,' Aunt Freda said, adding soothingly, 'Your sister took the children to Wanstead, when she saw you were too ill to receive her. Your mother is helping her to take care of them, and I expect Lady

Northumberland is enjoying the novelty, as she has no children of her own yet.'

'Three weeks!' Penelope said wonderingly. She allowed Aunt Freda to hold the glass of milk to her lips because when she tried to raise her hand it felt so heavy; it was easier to allow herself to be waited on.

This time, she drank half the milk before turning her head away.

'Now that you're taking nourishment you'll soon be strong again,' Aunt Freda said cheerfully, going over to a basin of water which stood on a joint stool near the fire, and rinsing the glass. 'When you are up, you may want to see the children for a while. I am sure Lord Rich will ride to Wanstead for them, when it is safe to do so.'

'Why safe? What has ailed me?' Penelope asked idly. In the little silence which followed, before Freda began to chatter unconvincingly of a fever, she looked at her arm lying on the coverlet. So thin and pale, like a stick of celery. Except for ugly, reddish brown blotches, faint enough, but still very much in evidence.

She felt a thrill of fear which blurred her vision for a moment, but she forced her eyes to focus on the spots, or whatever they were. Yes, they were spots, or rather pustulated blisters. She put her fingers onto the bare skin of her chest. She was so thin she could feel her bones but, unmistakably, the pustules were there too.

Freda had stopped talking and was watching her fearfully. 'It is smallpox, isn't it?' Penelope said heavily. 'Tell me the truth, Aunt Freda, or I shall get out of bed, weak as I am, to see for myself. Are there spots on my face?'

Freda began to sob, the thin, nervous hands coming up to cover her face.

Penelope leaned forward and laid her hand gently against the older woman's worn black sleeve.

'Don't be afraid, Aunt Freda, just tell

me,' she said with all the imperiousness she could muster.

Aunt Freda, shuddering and sobbing, did not attempt to answer her. But beneath the veil of her fingers Penelope saw the tear-drowned eyes open, and she gave a tremulous little nod.

* * * *

'Oh my dear Elizabeth, how good it is to see you! All the while I was ill poor Rich avoided me like the plague, and only Lavender and Aunt Freda Rich came near me. And to be honest, Rich was so nervous that I might still be carrying the disease that for many days I lived in the small parlour, dined there even, and he just used to pop his head round the door, ask after my health, and disappear.' She laughed. 'I could tell that he wouldn't draw breath whilst his head was in the room and I used to amuse myself, sometimes, by giving a protracted answer just to see his face turning purple.'

Elizabeth smiled affectionately at her cousin. 'To think of you being ill for weeks, and me not knowing,' she said. 'I would have come to you, Penny, and risked infection. But men are strange about sickness, more frightened than women. And how lucky you've been, my dear. Not a mark on you!'

'No, not even in the places you can't see,' Penelope admitted cheerfully. They were sitting in the formal garden, on cushions placed on the turf, and the warmth of the May sunshine brought flower perfumes, light but sweet, floating to them on the breeze.

Penelope glanced around them cautiously, then she leaned towards her cousin.

'I'll tell you one thing which the illness has taught me, Vernon. I have been wasting my life, and shall do so no more. When I am able to leave, I shall go to Charles.'

'Go to Mountjoy? Live openly with him?

Oh Penny, how can you? The Queen will be furious, and Essex will not be best pleased, and you will become a social outcast ...'

'Much I would care about that! But no, I can't go to him openly without losing my right to be with my children. I shall confide in my friends and relatives, and somehow, I shall manage to spend the best part of my life with Charles. You wait and see, I shall do it! These past weeks have been dreadful. We had no open link, he could not write to me nor I to him. Had I died, he would only have learned casually, from my brother perhaps, who knows we are very good friends. And if *he* were to die ...'

She broke off, remembering her agony of mind when she knew Philip was dying, far away from her.

Suddenly realising that Vernon was not totally in her confidence, she added, 'How did you know there was something between Charles and I, Elizabeth? We've confided in no-one.'

'I didn't know you were sleeping together, if that's what you mean, until you said "I shall go to Charles," and then I guessed, of course. If that is how you keep secrets, Penny, I shall be careful never to confide in you!'

'I must still be weak from the smallpox,' Penelope said. 'Now tell me, dear Vernon, how *is* Charles? Have you seen him?'

'Yes, I have. Penny, he is off to sea with your brother. Did you know that Robert is to lead another expedition to try to cripple Spanish shipping which is being built to send against England in another Armada?'

'I know nothing! Rich isn't interested in sea ventures, especially since he went with Essex on the Cadiz voyage, and found few pickings. Is your own lord sailing with them? And our other friends?'

'They will all go,' Elizabeth admitted. 'You know what Southampton is like, he would not miss an adventure with Essex for anything! And Rutland is just the same.'

'Then I shall have to improve, if I am to meet Charles before he sails, and tell him of my plans.' Penelope paused, thinking rapidly. 'Vernon, sweet Vernon, I must come back to London with you. We will contrive a tale which will keep Rich happy, and it will not be difficult. He could not see his latest mistress whilst I was here and ill in my bed, and now that I'm better he expects me to pick up my wifely burden again, but I am still too weak.' She sighed dramatically, rolling her eyes. 'So he will see me go with mixed feelings, poor creature.'

'I hope you will be strong enough, then, to say hello and goodbye to Charles in a satisfactory manner!'

Penelope pursed her lips, her eyes twinkling. 'I daresay I shall manage it.'

★ ★ ★ ★

Charles saw her coming down the cobbled street, from a window at the inn where they had agreed to meet. Despite the thick black shawl which she wore round her head, and the long cloak which covered her from chin to ankle, he knew her at once. That indefinably personal thing, one's walk, pinpointed her immediately.

He watched her arrival with a certain amount of amusement. When she reached the house she glanced up at the sign of the golden fleece, hanging on its creaking chain above the cobbles, and then she entered, moving so purposefully through the little group of idlers thronging the pavement that they gave way before her.

He slipped into the hall and saw her put back the shawl, revealing that golden guinea hair. She said in a small but clear voice, 'I want to see Mr Gray. Could you direct me to his room, please?'

The half-witted lad who was the landlord's dogsbody knew quality when he saw it, Charles noted with approval.

Without a word he dropped the heavy case he was supposed to be carrying up to one of the guest rooms, tugged his forelock, and beckoned with a blackened finger.

Penelope smiled at the urchin and followed him into the room which Charles had hired.

'He haint 'ere,' the boy muttered. 'But 'e haint likely to be long.'

'I'll wait,' Penelope said clearly. She saw the boy out and shut the door decisively.

Charles waited until the boy had disappeared into the back regions of the inn, then went as unobtrusively as he could to the door and slipped inside.

She ran into his arms and he kissed her fervently.

'Not a blemish on your skin, you perfect creature,' he said, holding her at arm's length. 'No wonder Sidney sang his most beautiful songs to you, and all the young men at court who can pen a line do likewise!'

'How pretty, Charles! But we haven't got long. I've come to bid you goodbye, of course. But when you come home again, I shall be with you. I must visit Rich, in order to keep up some semblance of respectability and to see the children, but I shall live with you. Oh, not openly, so that the Queen and all the court know—that would never do. I shall have to confide in the family, of course, and special friends. My brother keeps a suite of rooms for me at Essex House, the same suite which I used when it was Leicester House, oddly enough. We can live together there with no-one but family and trusted servants knowing, I assure you. And Wanstead is the same, and Chartley of course, and Drayton Bassett, which is mother's favourite country house. When Vernon marries Southampton, and she's bound to do so one day despite her Grace's displeasure, we can have rooms there, and one way and another we shall contrive, don't you think?'

'What cut-and-dried plans!' Charles said, half-laughing. 'But Penny, have you *told* these people about us? My dear, was that wise?'

She drew back a little, her eyes anxious. 'I've told Elizabeth Vernon, because I had to find out where you were and get a message to you. But no-one else knows. Charles, I can see you aren't pleased. I'm sorry. I always thought ...'

He interrupted her. 'My own love, of course I shall be pleased, when I get used to the idea. But men like to run down their own quarry, you know, and it is a trifle disconcerting to find you have planned the seduction of Rich's wife from his home and hearth, instead of me doing it for myself, as I'd planned.'

She smiled, cautiously hopeful. '*You* planned to do it? To lure me from my husband and children? And how had you worked it out, pray?'

'I had a chat to your brother. Essex said what a capital thing it was that I am already practically a member of the family—he meant Chris being his stepfather of course—because it would be relatively simple to arrange. He is giving me a room on the same floor as your suite, so we shall be respectable. And when we are in the country we can be even more together.'

She looked up at him, her eyes shining. 'Then you *are* willing?'

'Willing?' he said. With his forefinger he traced the line of her small nose, the dip of her upper lip, the line of her generous mouth. 'I am more than willing!'

'Rich is slow, but not totally stupid, and will realise that there is another man. But he won't complain as long as everything seems respectable.' She sighed. 'How I hate that word! But oh, take care of yourself during the voyage, my love! I've no desire to be a widow before I'm a common-law wife!'

He was not fooled by her matter-of-fact tone. He saw her lip tremble and knew that where he was concerned, she had no hardness, no practicality. She was moved only by love, she was all gentleness and generosity. Lovingly, he caught her in his arms and began to kiss her.

'Why did you not hire a bedroom whilst you were about it?' she said, as they sank onto the window seat.

'Too much money,' he retorted, grinning; then, relenting, 'there is a communicating door behind those hangings, with a boxy little bedroom on the other side. If you can wait until then, that is.'

She stood up, pulling him with her, and they went into the bedroom, their arms around each other. As soon as he had closed the door she turned in his arms and began rapidly unfastening her gown.

'I am without shame,' she said, her eyes laughing at him. 'It has been so long, Charles!'

★ ★ ★ ★

'You are an amazing woman, Pen! I miss

you so much when you are away, and yet as soon as you return from Leighs you are plunged into more work! I work hard, always have, yet compared to you I am an idle fellow.'

Penelope kissed Charles lightly. 'Nonsense,' she said gaily. 'If you must know, I thrive on my double life! My Rich children are happy and healthy, I've seen them for myself and therefore know that all is well there. I've got the books up-to-date, arranged the sale of the yearling lambs, had some repairs put in hand to cottages on the estate, and feel that all is in order at Leighs.'

'And now that I'm back at Wanstead with you, I can find out that my Blount children are well. They're all right, aren't they, Charles? I know you would have sent a message had little Mountjoy or baby Charles become poorly.'

'They are both well,' Charles said, smiling at her. 'And your mother has visited Chartley recently and is over the moon with them! The prettiest babies, she thinks them both, and the cleverest!'

'Then that's all right.' Penelope sighed, and pulled a chair up to Charles's desk. 'You were working when I arrived, so you had better begin again. I will sit here quietly and watch you until you've finished, and then we can talk.'

'I had finished, love. And we ought to talk at once. Have you seen Vernon yet? She and Henry are at Southampton House and I wondered whether you might have dropped in on her.'

'I came straight here,' Penelope said simply. 'Why do you ask?'

'Because there is trouble between Essex and the Queen. You know all about the rows they've had over the Islands voyage, when we missed the treasure fleet and failed to sink the second Armada; and then the row over the peace treaty with Spain. Burghley *knew* it was impossible for England to stand alone against the Spaniards but Essex still wants war.'

211

'I know all about *that*. But what is the latest business?'

Charles sighed. 'Essex wants to command the next army going to subdue Ireland. There has been so much trouble there, and the Queen wanted to appoint someone with more experience. But your brother shouts down every name which is put forward, save his own.'

'Well? Essex doesn't *really* want Ireland, Charles, he's not such a fool! That cannot be what is worrying you.'

'No, not entirely. Pen, sometimes I think Essex is mad! But I'll tell you the story and you may judge for yourself.'

And in simple language Charles told how Essex had suggested Carew, a friend of the Cecil's whom he hated, for the position of Lord Deputy of Ireland. The Queen, understanding all too well the reason for the choice, laughed and refused to listen. When Essex became angry and pushed his arguments to the point of absurdity, she lost her temper and began to shout back at him. Before any one could move or protest, Essex leaped to his feet with an exclamation and deliberately turned his back on the Queen.

'She boxed his ears, Pen, and who could blame her? Essex whirled round, his hand flying to his sword hilt, and had it half out of its sheath before you could say knife!'

'The crazy fool,' Penelope breathed.

'Yes. Nottingham got between them but could not prevent Essex from shouting defiance at the Queen as he was hustled from the room. Elizabeth just stood, white-faced, and watched him go.'

'So that is why he's not here to welcome me. Is he in the Tower?'

Charles grinned and shrugged. 'No. I will say this for him, he must be better loved by the Queen than one would guess. He took himself off down to Wanstead and there he stays, sulking, refusing to accept visits from the Queen's representatives, apparently waiting for Elizabeth to send an abject apology for daring to be annoyed that he should draw his sword in her presence.'

'Someone will have to speak to him,' Penelope said gloomily. 'He is the most marvellous person—generous, easy-going, and sweet-tempered—unless crossed.'

'But everyone who does not agree instantly with every word he says, is counted an enemy now, Pen. He is changing. I will escort you down to Wanstead in a day or two, and you can see for yourself. If he consents to see us, that is!'

★ ★ ★ ★

But the months wore on, and the chance for a serious talk with Essex did not arise. For one thing, no-one who wanted to remain his friend fancied the thought of trying to disagree with him. The secretary, Francis Bacon, who might have done it, had long left Essex House, to seek his fortune with a less flamboyant but more mature patron.

Charles had spoken to Essex's especial cronies, Southampton, Rutland, the unpleasant Danvers brothers who owed their necks to Essex—he had extricated one of them at least from an unpleasant murder-charge. Even Gelli Meyrick and Anthony Bagot, both very old friends, hesitated to question their leader's wisdom in so openly defying the Queen.

'It is not that Gelli dare not, but that he sees nothing wrong in *anything* Essex does or says,' Penelope said bitterly to Elizabeth Vernon. 'And your husband, who is in trouble with the Queen anyway for having married you, is no better! He should be trying to keep in Elizabeth's good books, instead of aiding and abetting my brother in everything he undertakes.'

The two friends had been visiting the court and were being rowed back to Essex House along the Thames. It was a pleasant afternoon in late autumn, and the breeze which wafted to them across the face of the water was a nice change from the stuffier atmosphere on land.

'Has it never occurred to you, Penny, that though Essex does and says things which seem incredibly foolish and foolhardy, he always seems to win his way back into the Queen's favour? I've talked it over with my dear Henry, and he is sure that Essex has the right of it; that Elizabeth really rather *likes* to have a man shouting at her and making her bend, just a little, to suit him instead of it always being the other way around. Henry thinks that perhaps we would do better to let Essex handle the Queen, since he seems able to do it to such advantage.'

'Maybe you're right,' Penelope said. 'Did you know I'm in correspondence with Jamie of Scotland, Vernon? And sometimes, when I am penning a letter, I say a little private prayer. I pray that James comes to the throne soon enough to save Essex from committing some fault that she will *not* wink at.'

★ ★ ★ ★

'Why do you want to talk to me, Penny? Goodness knows, you've talked to me often enough!'

Robert switched moodily with his stick at the low branches of the apple trees, then with a sudden change of mood, bent and picked a newly flowering daffodil and stuck it in his doublet.

'Because I want to tell you that I've accepted the Queen's offer of a post in her household; well, that sounds rather important, but she wants me to go to court again, as one of her ladies in waiting.'

'Nice for you.'

'No, brother. Nice for you! I have said I will go merely because you will be in Ireland at the head of your troops, and I thought it might be of assistance to you to learn court gossip from me when I write. After all, most of your close friends will be going to Ireland with you.'

'Good of you,' Essex said shortly. 'I wish I had not got to go! Ireland is a hard place for a man to make a name for himself.'

Penelope forbore telling him that he alone was responsible for his present predicament, but said stoutly, 'You made your name on the Cadiz venture, Essex! In Ireland you have merely to consolidate the good impression all England has of you. You must show them all that you can command men to good effect.'

'And at home, Penny, they will be free to work against me. Oh, I know there are those who though they smile into my face now, will rend me as soon as my back is turned! They think me a simple fellow, but I've noted them.'

'Who?' Penelope said baldly. 'Name me some names.'

Essex blinked at her, then said vaguely, 'It doesn't do to point at one more than another. You would not realise, being a woman, but there is treachery in all.'

'In Charles, would you say?'

He blinked again, looking sulky and defensive.

'Not Charles, of course not Charles. *He* is loyal enough. Though I've no doubt he wanted to go to Ireland as Lord Deputy, in his heart. But I talked them out of sending him.' He chuckled. 'That pleased you didn't it, pretty sister? You would sooner see me go than your lover, I'm sure of that!'

'Does that mean you think I am disloyal?'

'Don't be ridiculous! Why, I'd as soon doubt my mother! No, it is others who would bring me down if they could.'

'Ralegh? Cecil? The Queen herself, maybe?'

Essex smiled condescendingly. 'Pah! The Queen is a mere woman, when all's said and done. She was made to be persuaded, as any woman is. No, it is the persuaders whom I fear. Cecil, yes, and Ralegh. All that crew. And others, closer to me.'

They had reached the end of the orchard

now, and Essex swung round and headed back towards the house so fast that Penelope had to trot to keep up.

Glancing back at her and shamefacedly slowing his pace, he said gruffly, 'Sorry, but I want an early night. We leave soon after dawn tomorrow, and I should like to get a good way before we stop for the night. Will you be up to see me off?'

Something in his anxious smile brought the old days flooding back; the days when the little brother had cried to Penny to lift him up to see the haymakers through the nursery window, begged her, hoping, to let him have a try with the long-bow she was just learning to bend. Then, his jealous rages had been saved for baby brother Walter, who got too much of nurse's attention, or for his mother when she forbade some enterprising new venture.

She thought ruefully that Essex had always overshadowed Walter; had in the end caused his death by taking him out to France and teasing him into parading around the walls of Rouen, when a sniper's bullet had taken him in the head. All for vanity, she thought.

But Walter had ceased to be a menace to Essex long before his death. He had been a quiet, studious boy totally uninterested in court life, enjoying Chartley and the country things he knew so well.

And what was the menace to him now? She tried to tell herself it was Cecil, Ralegh, the Howards, but in her heart she knew the answer. It was his own nature.

TEN

The mare was fresh, and would have liked to canter through the busy streets, but Penelope held her to a trot. For though she wanted with all her heart to hurry, she knew that it might prove dangerous to be seen riding fast away from Nonsuch towards Essex House.

For Essex was home at last! He had been half a year in Ireland, and he had failed to bring the country back under the English yoke. How dismally he had failed, she could only guess from the strange manner of his unexpected arrival.

She and two other women in attendance upon the Queen that morning had been busy in the Privy Chamber and the wardrobe, preparing the Queen's gown, pouring her a drink of hot milk, splashing rose water, tidying up after the night. She had been busy, and happy, for her tasks were light ones compared with the disciplining and child-rearing in which she had recently been engaged at Leighs. Her daughters were growing up, Letty and the young Penelope, known as Lally at home, were half-help, half-hindrance.

Humming as she folded a cast-off shawl, she had turned away from the clothes chest to see the door burst open, without so much a knock. A tall man in riding clothes, wild and unkempt, entered the room. She had recognised her brother with horror—a man in the Queen's room before she was dressed was terrible enough, but that it should be Essex, whom she had believed in Ireland!

For once, her competence left her; she gaped as incredulously as the other women and when the Queen gestured at them to leave the room she hastened to obey, her mind in a turmoil.

But outside the door she had dropped to her knees, applying her ear unashamedly to the keyhole, listening to the murmur of voices. The Queen spoke once or twice, in a gentle friendly way. Penelope thought of her cropped grey head waiting for the beautifully groomed wig, of the sagging face without its make-up, and swallowed. Once again, it would seem, her brother's indiscretion had come at the right moment. For a miracle, she was not angry!

Then Essex talked for a longer time— explaining, complaining, his deep voice going on and on, becoming petulant, at times almost shrill, until Penelope could have screamed at the unwisdom of it.

Then she only just had time to scuttle back a reasonable distance when the door opened, and Essex came out. He smiled at his sister without surprise.

'Can I come to your apartments and clean up?' he said. 'Penny, I *knew* it would be all right if only I could explain to her by myself! I knew she would understand that nothing was *my* fault, that I was the victim of ... well, of a thousand different things. She was so good, so understanding!'

He had allowed Penelope to lead him to her room, his tired, haunted face almost content.

'I am to speak to the Queen at greater length when we are both more presentable,' he said in reply to her questions. 'I cannot tell you any more, yet. But would you do something for me?'

'Of course.'

'Tell my friends to come to Nonsuch. I

daresay they're all in London at present. Of course my travelling companions will stand by me, and remain with me here. But I would like the others to come.'

'Very well. Rich is staying with friends; I can tell him. And Charles, of course. Francis Bacon is visiting his brother Anthony, so he will probably be at Essex House. And Rutland is in Town. But Essex, what will be thought if I ride out myself? Would it not be better to send a messenger, in case the Queen dislikes the thought that you are sending for your—your allies?'

He was immediately contemptuous, flicking his hand dismissively. 'I will persuade the Queen that I want my friends with me, in case Cecil and the others try to outmanoeuvre me. Be a good girl and be my messenger.'

She could only agree.

And luck was with her. At the very doorway of Essex House was a jovial party of men, just setting out for a ride.

Rich, Rutland and Charles were mounted, Francis Bacon and Lord Sandys were on foot, obviously seeing the party away.

She reined in her mount, smiled, and said 'He is home! At Nonsuch,' and the words were all they needed. To a man they wheeled their horses and Bacon shouted at the groom to get off so that he might use his mount.

Old Lord Sandys danced with fury at being left, but he could not ride the mare Penelope had brought with the side-saddle still up. Instead he ran round to the stables like a man half his age, and as Penelope handed the mare to a groom she could hear the old gentleman frantically bellowing at a stable boy to saddle him a fresh horse.

By the time she had returned to the house, she could hear his horse's hooves clattering over the driveway.

★ ★ ★ ★

'He carried all before him at the second

meeting, Pen! Nothing could have been happier than his demeanour when he came out of the Privy Chamber. But I should have guessed something was wrong when we dined. The Cecil faction ate apart from us, with long faces. They made it plain they thought Essex was in for trouble. And by God, how right they were! After we'd eaten, she called him in for yet another audience. It was pathetic, in a way. He bounced in, eyes bright, going to conquer once more; you could see what he thought by his walk alone. Then he came out—but how changed! His face was red, whether from rage or embarrassment I couldn't tell. He had been excusing his conduct in leaving Ireland for an hour, we could hear his voice rising to a shout through the door.

'He is confined to his room at Nonsuch Palace until the Queen has made up her mind what to do with him.'

Penelope's face was serious. 'What *did* happen in Ireland, Charles? Have you managed to discover the truth of it.'

'I spoke to Chris, who is hot in defence of your brother, of course. But from what he told me, such foolishness has been perpetrated! The army slogged across country, losing men from desertion, being ambushed, falling ill, and they took not one town to hold and keep, they destroyed not one nest of the rebels! A town would welcome them with cheering, put out the flags for them, and even as they marched out the citizens would be welcoming Tyrone's rebels in by the other gate! If they have gates, which I doubt, but you know what I mean. As if that weren't bad enough, Essex met with Tyrone and agreed a peace treaty with him which is little short of disaster. The promises your brother made! If the Queen were not so fond of him, and if it would not implicate so many, the word "treason" might well be used towards him.'

In the quiet of their bedroom, the word lost little of its sinister meaning.

'Treason!'

'Pen, he promised that the Irish may remain in possession of everything they held on the 8th September, which is to say virtually everything; he swore we would not establish any new garrisons or forts. There is to be a truce, which either side may break at fourteen days' notice—see how advantageous that is to Tyrone! He is there, on the spot, with the Irish hordes only waiting for the word to rally to him, whereas we have to bring an army across the Irish sea—*and* Tyrone is expecting a Spanish force to arrive any time now from Philip, to help fight us. The Queen sent him to subdue Ireland, not to lose half his men through illness and inefficiency and then to crawl to Tyrone, agreeing to monstrous terms in her name, and then run back home again!'

'He has been a fool, but *not* a villain. I hope to God she understands that. What will happen, Charles? Will he be sent back to Ireland? If so, I cannot see him undoing

229

the harm he has done! Though some of the men will be loyal—they love him, do they not?'

'Those men whom he has knighted will doubtless stand by him,' Charles said evasively. 'But darling, he knighted over eighty! The Queen is furious, naturally, she has been so careful of the honours she gives. Essex should never have been sent, though, she should have ignored his pleadings and plottings.'

'But now, Charles. What is to happen *now?*' You know how I love my brother, but I can still see his faults and failings. He knows nothing of strategy or guile. If only the Queen will understand this and let him have his place at court once more!'

Charles grimaced. 'Only time will tell, but she's never allowed her anger to outlast her love of him before. Let's go to bed now, sweet, it's been a long day.'

★ ★ ★ ★

Penelope, Elizabeth, Countess of South-ampton and Frances, Essex's wife, were standing around the long table in the hall at Essex House, sorting out their New Year gifts. Lists of purchases still to be made, piles of discarded oddments for the servants, and the bits and pieces for their numerous children were piled on the board, but though their hands were busy, their minds were far from the mundane task.

'Now that Essex is under the Lord Keeper Egerton's guardianship, at York House, I should have thought I might be allowed to see him. But no, the Queen does not approve of wives.'

'Don't be bitter, Frances. When the baby is old enough to take it visiting, there is your excuse! Not even the Queen would be cruel enough to deny a father's right to see his child,' Penelope said. 'Vernon, would your daughter like these pearls? I always think pearls are so nice for young girls, and these are rather good ones.'

Elizabeth Vernon held out her hand for the pearls and began to reply when a servant entered the room.

'Some gentlemen to see Lady Essex or Lady Rich,' the man said resignedly. 'Military gentlemen, again.'

Hard at his heel a group of shabby men entered the room, staring curiously at the glittering piles on the table, and at the grandly dressed ladies.

'I'm Lady Rich,' Penelope said, smiling at them. 'Lady Essex has recently borne her husband a child, and is still weak.'

The half-lie had been agreed between her and Frances, for the younger woman did not feel herself capable of dealing with the numerous calls from those interested in the Earl's welfare.

'How is the Earl keeping milady?' said the man who had obviously been voted their spokesman. 'We've come back from Ireland for a spell, for we've mostly been ill, as the Earl has.'

'Essex is still far from well,' Penelope said. 'He is at York House, you know, but the Queen will not allow him to see visitors, or I'm sure he would have gladly spoken with you of your ...'

One of the younger men interrupted her without ceremony.

'We *did* get permission, milady,' he said eagerly. 'On account of having despatches and personal letters for the Earl. But he would not see us! Lord Keeper Egerton tried to persuade him, but he wouldn't even take the letters. So the Lord Keeper handed them back to us, very sorrowful, and said the Earl was in a black mood and had had the misfortune beside to fall prey to an 'eadache and we'd best deliver the letters to you.'

'Oh!' Penelope said, taken aback. 'Well, as I said he has been ill, and no doubt fears to pass infection on, perhaps.' She took the bundle of letters, eyeing them uncertainly. 'I'll see that these are ... are dealt with. And if you meet other men who want

233

word of the Earl, would you send them to me? Morgan!'

The servant came running at her call.

'Give these men a drink and a bite in the kitchen, so that they can drink the Earl's health. Good-day to you.'

They left the room, and Penelope's false calm deserted her.

'Good God, what is he up to now! Why did he risk antagonising those men? Why would he not at least accept the letters? I suppose he is sulking again, and what a foolish time to choose! I am almost out of patience with him!'

★ ★ ★ ★

Essex continued to carry out a protracted sulk in York House and Penelope very soon regretted her generous impulse to invite chance-met soldiers to visit her. They besieged the house. From the moment she came down the stairs in the morning to the moment she climbed them at night, a host of men were knocking at her door.

The young Southamptons were towers of strength, though Penelope suspected that many times Henry closeted men with him in Essex's study to talk something approaching sedition.

Rich was staying at Essex House so Charles had moved back into lodgings. They met sometimes, but had little time for private conversation.

'Essex is genuinely ill now,' Charles told her. 'That is why the Queen is going to send him back to Essex House and that is a blessing, because if you don't move down to Wanstead and get some peace, you'll be ill.'

'And what of Ireland?' Penelope asked suspiciously. 'Are you still holding out against the Queen's wish that you go to Ireland in Essex's stead. My darling, I could not bear to see you, too, defeated by that confounded country.'

'If I went, I might defeat Ireland,' Charles said. 'But I'm still saying "no" as politely as I can. But I hope you realise, my darling, that if she should insist, I cannot refuse.'

'All my reliance is upon you,' Penelope said, tears rising to her eyes. 'And my brother's too. If you do badly and are killed, I shall die too, and if you do well then you will shame Essex and finish him in the Queen's eyes. You must find a way to refuse, Charles!'

'Dearly though I love you, I cannot fail in Ireland just to save your brother's reputation. And as a commander of men, his reputation is not worth the saving, to be blunt with you. Rest assured, however, that I am no more keen to face the cold and misery of an Irish campaign than you are to see me go. And now go I must! Goodnight, darling!'

★ ★ ★ ★

With Charles in Ireland, there was no-one to stop Penelope, in a mood of despair, entering the lists in her brother's defence. Recklessly, she wrote to the Queen, larding the letter with ridiculous, effusive compliments on the Queen's legendary beauty. To a woman of over sixty, the letter was an insult. Penelope was hailed before the Council to account for herself, and upon being remonstrated for the tone of the letter, she grew tight-lipped, and refused to explain further than saying, 'What I meant, I wrote, and what I wrote, I meant.'

'Because of your pig-headedness,' Frances said to her furiously, 'I am forbidden to see my husband for more than a few hours. Oh, Penny, the Queen was relenting, you know she was! I've been spending all day at York House, cheering him up, taking the baby with me so that he could play with the child, and now this!'

'Well, I'm under house arrest here, and may not go out,' Penelope said sulkily, indicating the confines of Essex House. 'Charles said *weeks* ago that Essex was

237

to be brought here, so I packed and moved down to Wanstead and nothing happened.'

'Something is happening now! He *is* coming to Essex House, and you are to move down to Wanstead, still under house arrest. I shan't come, I shall move back into Walsingham House with the children until the summer, anyway.'

Penelope suddenly jumped to her feet and flung her arms around Frances.

'Frances, I am sorry! Forgive me for acting like a spoilt child! But I miss Charles desperately, I've not seen Essex once, not even for a moment, since he was first sent to York House, and I *know* my interference did nothing but harm. I feel so guilty and miserable!'

'Oh, well,' Frances said, 'I know you love Essex really, Penny, and would do him no deliberate harm. Let's kiss and make up.'

★ ★ ★ ★

Penelope sat in the lady chamber at Leighs, paper spread out before her, writing to Charles. Outside, the hot summer sun fell on the heads of five of her seven children, who were playing at target shooting; the older girls were working in the house with Aunt Freda Rich, growing older but still capable.

So much had happened, Penelope thought, since Charles had gone to Ireland. There had been her disgrace over that wretched letter; she had been under house arrest, unable to receive visitors, supposed not to write letters, from the middle of January until the end of August. Then the Council had met in York House to judge her brother's actions.

Francis Bacon, one time secretary and friend of Essex, had led the prosecution. But though the blame had been placed firmly upon Essex's shoulders, the Council had really done nothing. Essex was to

239

remain a prisoner at Essex House with Sir Richard Berkeley as his jailer, and she was to remain at Wanstead, able to walk in the gardens but still not able to leave the grounds.

During all this time, her brother had been ill to varying degrees. The Irish flux had never left him totally, and was apt to recur whenever he was depressed.

After the trial, his illness increased and by the end of August, he was so weak that the Queen relented to the extent of allowing him to go down to his uncle's home, Ewelme Lodge, with Frances and Lettice and other friends and relatives. She had also lifted her ban on Penelope.

Penelope had immediately decided to join her brother at Ewelme Lodge, had even penned a hurried note to Charles telling him of her decision, when a messenger had arrived, changing her plans completely.

He had come from Leighs, with a curt note from Letty. 'Father is ill. Can you come?'

Knowing her daughter's efficiency, and knowing also the burden which her own defection laid upon shoulders too young to be so laden, Penelope had not hesitated but had ridden down to Leighs at once.

Letty had not exaggerated. She entered the house to find it hushed, the children huddled in corners, afraid to play, the whole atmosphere redolent of sickness.

She soon changed all that. She sent the children into the gardens, telling them to spend as much time as possible in the open air. She chased Aunt Freda into her own room to sleep, and she took over the nursing of her husband.

Tiptoeing into his room she saw that he had aged; his square, unimaginative face was thinner now, the cheeks hollow, and his hair was beginning to recede, giving him a false air of intelligence with the higher forehead. He opened his eyes and she saw them dull, absorbed in his discomfort, indifferent to others.

'Robert?' she said gently. 'Robert? It is

me, Penelope, come to take care of you.'

He nodded, very slowly, then said, 'Penny? You've come? Letty said you would. You'll soon pull me round.'

And she read the pleasure and trust which shone in his eyes and knew that despite her failures towards him, she was still very welcome.

She had pulled him round, by a dint of devoting every minute to him for many days. She was glad that he was better; it seemed that despite his many faults a trace of tenderness towards him remained in her heart.

But reminiscing was not helping to get her letters written! She squared her elbows and began to write steadily.

★ ★ ★ ★

'I am going back to London tomorrow, Letty my dear. You and Lally have been marvellous, I could never have managed without you. I should love to take you both back to Essex House with me, but it would not be wise at present. I hope that, perhaps in the spring, you will be able to visit me, though. It is time you met young men and had some fun.'

Letty was sitting on her mother's bed, rocking idly from side to side and watching Lavender carefully fold the gowns which Penelope handed to her.

'Is it because your lover is in London that we cannot return with you?'

Penelope felt her eyes widen. 'No, it is not,' she said. 'What do you know of my lover, miss?'

Not at all discomposed, Letty said airily, 'Nothing, save that you have one! And why not? Father has his women, doesn't he? We miss you so much, mother, when you go away but Lally and I have always comforted ourselves by saying that you've gone back to the man who makes you happy, and does not ill-treat you as father did.'

Penelope felt tears rise to her eyes, and

bent her head, furiously blinking.

'You're a good girl, Letty. And Lally is another. I shall be back to see you and the little ones soon enough. Not that any of you are little now! Great creatures, how you make me feel my age!' She paused, then took another dress off its hook. 'Continue to think kindly of me,' she whispered.

ELEVEN

She had never seen Essex House so crowded. For a moment she had been frightened, had almost wheeled her horse around and fled, for the courtyard was packed with retainers, messengers and old soldiers.

Then she relaxed, and led her horse round to the stables. Of course, it was the first time Essex had been free in

London since his return from Ireland—no, since he had first set off for Ireland—and that had been the best part of two years. Of course the people were delighted to see him home, and had flocked to tell him so.

She strolled into the house, her face pink from the crispness of the winter air, to find her mother organising everyone with enthusiasm.

'Penny! You're here at last! How's Rich? Have you brought him with you?'

'He's much better, but he won't be travelling far from Leighs this winter. He's weak still, and is best quietly at home, I'm happy to say. Not that it matters much, with Charles still in Ireland. But mother, what is all the excitement about? I had a letter from Essex, suggesting that I might return to London, but he said nothing more.'

Lettice clicked with vexation. 'There! Stupid boy, I might have known he would leave the most important part of the message out. Sit down by the fire, Penny, and I'll tell you.'

Penelope listened. Essex, his mother told her, was financially at rock-bottom. His grants and favours had all come from the Queen, and she would no longer renew them. He was out of favour and forbidden to come to the court, so he could see no chance of getting back into favour again by fair means.

'He wrote to Mountjoy, asking him to bring back the army from Ireland to replace him by force in the Queen's favour, but Charles prevaricates,' Lettice said. 'Of course, it isn't Elizabeth who denies him favours really, it is Cecil, Ralegh, and the rest of that crew. Why, Essex says he knows for a fact that Cecil is plotting to see the succession goes, not to James, but to the Spanish Infanta. What do you think about that?'

That shot certainly went home. Penelope had for some years, as a sort of insurance, been exchanging letters with King James of Scotland. She used code, of course, her own name being Ryalta for such purposes, but nevertheless James would know Ryalta was Penelope Rich as soon as he set eyes on her, for she had sent her portrait a year ago, and had received his compliments upon her pretty face.

But suppose her mother was right, and Cecil *was* angling for the Spanish succession? Her future, and Charles's and Essex's, to say nothing of half the court who had also corresponded with James, would be dark indeed.

'Why *did* you send for me then?' Penelope asked. 'Can I help you, since Charles cannot?' She saw her mother's sardonic look and added hastily, 'Do not think him disloyal to Essex, but how *could* he bring an army against the Queen? Even if it was said afterwards that he did it for James, what monarch could trust a soldier who used his troops for such a doubtful purpose?'

'That is true,' nodded Lettice. 'Well

then, we will forgive Charles if you will be messenger for us in his stead. You know all my son's friends, and where they live; you even know many of the soldiers who felt they'd had a bad deal over the Irish business and came home to England to lie low. It is these people we want contacted.

'We cannot send men of importance, for they would be immediately suspected. But who suspects a woman? At best, they will think you are making up for the time you lost by being put under house arrest last year, and are living in a whirl of society gaiety; at worst, that you've taken innumerable lovers. What they *won't* think is that you are gathering your brother's allies together!'

'Of course I'll do it,' Penelope said. 'I shall be proud!'

★ ★ ★ ★

The exciting, dangerous days passed.

Penelope rode on a dun pony muffled up to her eyes, visiting the strangest places; little inns where they treated her with awe and a sort of leering respect, farms where she had to lift her skirts almost to her knees to avoid the dung which littered the entrance, huge mansions where she entered undisguised, as of right—and was then closeted in the master's study, talking, talking, far into the night.

And because of her excursions, Essex House overflowed with men who were rallying around Essex. The Southamptons moved out of stately Southampton House and in with the Devereux, so that their own mansion might be taken over by the supporters who had nowhere else to lay their heads.

'I've been too busy even to drop Charles a line since I came to London,' Penelope said to Elizabeth Vernon. 'I just hope it is all worthwhile, that James does come to the throne, and that, somehow, the Queen is persuaded to forgive Essex and grant him enough money to live on!'

'I wouldn't do what you are doing for a thousand times a thousand pounds,' Elizabeth said, shivering. 'You must have travelled hundreds of miles on that pony, and on foot, these past few days! and the places you've been—dirty cottages with deserters living in every nook and cranny, and none too careful who they hit over the head, either, and little shops where the apprentices are known to be malcontents, and inns where they've been in trouble for watering the beer ...'

'Spare me a list of them,' begged Penelope. 'Believe me, I dream abut some of my visits! Yesterday a drunken old fool almost cut my throat because I tried to step over him where he lay on the cobbles, and managed somehow to tread on his hand. As if I'd do such a foolish thing on purpose, but it was all I could do to convince him.'

'How did you do it in the end? Convince him, I mean?'

'Well, a crowd had gathered,' Penelope said, smiling to herself. 'And they were all on his side, mind you, stupid creatures! I was getting quite desperate, when suddenly I pushed back my hood the better to convince them that I was not some official or other disguised as a woman. My hair tumbled down, and someone said, "Swelp me, if it ain't Sidney's wench!"'

'By the grace of God, it was a butler who had served with the Sidney family years ago, and he had been in Philip's employ until his death. What a coincidence, eh?'

'Yes, but did that mend matters?'

'Well, not exactly. But then I had my brainwave, and I said, in my best theatrical tones, "And Essex's sister!", and then I pushed my dark cloak aside so that everyone could see my scarlet gown with the cream lace, and I smiled. The old villain let go my shoulder and put away his dagger, and the crowd shouted at him, and he patted my shoulder, and showed me the way to my destination.'

'Put away his *dagger?* Dear God, Penny, then he really might have killed you!'

'Of course! Why else do you think I have nightmares?'

★ ★ ★ ★

Penelope lay in the darkness, with Elizabeth Vernon on one side of her and Frances on the other. The room was crowded, for Essex had given up his bedroom to the women of his family and here they were all sleeping tonight, crowded in three beds and half a dozen straw pallets, because every room in the house was full. Penelope craned her neck and strained her eyes to see the window. Already she fancied she could discern a lightening of the darkness. Soon, too soon it seemed to her, day would dawn. Already she could hear the faint murmur of voices as somewhere in the house, men began to prepare for the day which lay ahead.

For it had come to a head at last, this

mad adventure. And in a way, it had been brought to a head by the very body of men who had been doing their utmost to prevent it; the Council themselves.

Last evening, secretary Herbert had been despatched by the Council to find out what was going on at Essex House. The crowds of men, particularly soldiers, the Welsh conscripted by busy Gelli Meyrick, the Irish rebels, Penelope's own contribution of the malcontents of the London gutters, had become so numerous that it was obvious to everyone that something was brewing at Essex House.

Secretary Herbert had been admitted and had requested Essex to present himself at once before the Privy Council. Essex, knowing how near he was to beginning his action, prevaricated. He was unwell, he had enemies who wished him harm. He would be pleased to appear before their lordships when he was well again.

But though he had not been indiscreet enough to go to court or to tell Herbert anything, this meant that action could no longer be delayed. At the council of war which Essex called, it was decided that they must act the following day or lose their chance for ever. The court was at the Palace of Whitehall, so they would attack there, and then they would go to the Tower of London, where the artillery was kept. But first, they would march upon the city, where a certain Sheriff Smyth had promised them the support of a thousand men.

There are men in plenty willing to fight for Essex, Penelope told herself, as the pale dawn light strengthened outside the window. They are ill-armed, but willing. What of the thousand men in the city? Would they bear arms? Her uneasiness, it seemed, grew with the daylight. If only Charles were here to give good counsel, she thought. But he is not, and Southampton and Rutland are straws which bend when Essex touches them. Bedford, Sandys, the Danvers brothers, Meyrick ...

She ran through the names in her head. All followers, all men who needed money desperately badly, all men who wanted James on the throne when Elizabeth dies.

She began to think of the men who would stand against Essex when he marched his motley crew against the palace. Cecil, Ralegh, Howard; all men of position and good reputation, who were established already in the government of the country.

Someone passed by her door and a hand knocked lightly against the panel, whether intentionally or by accident she could not tell. Elizabeth stirred, and on one of the straw pallets Lady Rutland, Philip Sidney's daughter Fanny, asked in a sleep blurred voice if it was time to rise yet.

Penelope waited for a moment, then slipped cautiously out of bed, stepping over Fanny's pallet. It was a bitterly cold morning. Shivering, she began to dress. Minutes later, she pulled open the door and began to trot down the corridor. As she had guessed, the house was awake. She began to descend the stairs. In the hall below she could see the top of Essex's chestnut head as he strode about, giving orders and countermanding them the next minute. Beside him Gelli trotted, a list in his hand, his hair dishevelled.

Essex heard her descending the stairs and turned to grin up at her.

'*Good* morning, Penny,' he said jovially. 'Believe it or not, there's a visitor outside.'

'Already?' Penelope said with an attempt at lightness. 'Who can be calling so early?'

'Only Ralegh! He wants to speak with Gorges, who is a relative of his I believe. They're together now.'

'You've left them alone together? Was that wise?'

Penelope knew that Sir Ferdinand Gorges, Governor of Plymouth, had family connections with the Raleghs and the Carews, and that they all came from the same part of Devonshire. She realised that Gorges was a weak man, and easily swayed;

his shilly-shallying had already brought Southampton's wrath down on his head.

'I'm not that foolish,' Essex said. 'They have met in two boats, on the Thames outside. Chris would like to shoot Ralegh like a sitting duck, and finish off at least one member of the Cecil faction. But they are under his eye, even if I'll not countenance plain murder.'

'And Gorges is coming back now, he's reached the landing stage,' Southampton said. He had been outside and entered, fresh-faced from the cold air. With his golden hair gleaming from a recent brushing and his cheeks pink, he looked the very picture of innocent amiability. Penelope was not the only one to know how his nature belied his sunny looks!

Essex swung round. 'What did they say?' he demanded. 'I couldn't hear much of what Ralegh said, just something about being a fool and accompanying him before it was too late. All Gorges said was, 'You are like to have a bloody day of it'. Then he just sat listening, with his mouth shut, and then rowed back to us and Ralegh sculled off up-river.'

'Good, good,' Essex said. He turned back to his sister. 'Go and rouse the women, there's a good girl, and then help the servants to give us all a bite before we leave.'

He smiled at her, then said in a bellow, 'All who own horses, join me in my study.'

There was a surge and a rush, and Penelope went thoughtfully back upstairs.

★ ★ ★ ★

'They've gone,' Penelope said. She had rushed out of the house behind them, watching their progress down the Strand towards the city. At first she had been as puzzled as some of the servants who were remaining behind, but then she remembered Sheriff Smyth and the reinforcements. Of course, they would march to the city first and then on to Whitehall and the Tower.

Just inside the hall was Anthony Bacon. A cripple, but one of the most intelligent and likeable men she had ever known. She had liked him from their first meeting as instinctively as she had disliked his brother Francis.

'They are mad!' he said now, distractedly. 'Mad! Lady Rich, I tell you that if Lord Mountjoy were here he would never have allowed you to lend yourself to such folly. I wish I'd more influence with my lord Essex, indeed I do, but he would never listen to me, not when he wouldn't listen to Francis.'

'We only have one life, Anthony,' Penelope said uncomfortably. 'And without the Queen's favour, what would my brother's life be? All his money has been spent on the Irish campaign, on the Islands voyage, and before that in France and the Netherlands. All for the Queen! And now that she no longer holds him in affection, can he live on air? She will not forgive his debts to her. This action has not been undertaken merely from a wish to regain his place at court, but to give him the means to live! And, perhaps almost more important, to ensure the succession of James of Scotland.'

'You may tell that, Lady Rich, to the gentlemen being held against their will in the study! They are good Protestants, every one, as is Robert Cecil.'

'Oh, lord, yes! For one happy moment, I'd forgotten them. But what alternative had we? Having got through the crowd in the courtyard—and I thought every moment to see them knifed, or clubbed by one of those ruffians—Essex could scarcely go back with them to meet the Privy Council, nor could he allow them to return to the Palace to tell Cecil what was afoot.'

'But how long do you think the Council will wait for their messengers' return? How long before they become suspicious and begin arming themselves against Essex?'

'Unless they are fools, they will arm within the hour,' Penelope admitted. 'But surely by then my brother will have met with Smyth and his reinforcements and marched on Whitehall?' She smiled at Anthony, guessing from his stricken expression how his loyalties were being torn. 'Cheer up! After all, Essex is not going to kill anyone, nor will he allow his followers to do so. At Whitehall he will take prisoner Ralegh, Cecil, and those other ambitious men who would stop him seeing the Queen. And once Elizabeth has seen him, can you imagine her not forgiving him? He looks so bright and confident this morning. He will charm her once more, you'll see! And when she is in his pocket again, he will make her sign a document regarding the succession.'

'You cannot charm at swordpoint, not even Essex could,' Anthony said stubbornly. 'And can Essex control *all* his men, Lady Rich? Your mother's husband,

Chris Blount, now there's a violent man! Ah, I know he's Mountjoy's brother but they are different as chalk from cheese. There is little good in Chris Blount, and much malice. And you must know that there are those in his train who would harm the Queen herself, if chance came their way.'

'I hope to God you're wrong,' Penelope said. 'But they've gone now, and we can only wait on events. I am going to help the women clear up after the huge breakfast which we served lately.'

In the kitchens, the women were still clearing dishes and washing them. Penelope joined them. Frances and her daughter, Lady Rutland, were up to their elbows in greasy water, whilst a couple of maidservants cleared the scraps off the plates before handing them over to be washed and two more piled the clean dishes up and took them away.

'Phew, I'm glad I wasn't born a kitchen maid,' Frances remarked, wiping the perspiration off her brow with her wrist. 'How are you getting on, Fanny?'

Her daughter heaved a sigh. 'Slowly,' she admitted. 'Would you like to wash up for a change, Aunt Penelope?'

Penelope, laughing, declined.

'And I am going to carry away your helper,' she declared. 'Frances, will you come with me? I thought I might go up to Essex's study and talk to the men imprisoned there. It can do no harm, and might do a deal of good.'

She glanced round the room, suddenly missing someone. 'Where is my mother?'

'She's gone, Penny, with the other women. She is going to Walsingham House to keep an eye on my children and she's taken Elizabeth Vernon with her. I think it is for the best. God knows where we shall be or in what state when this day ends.'

Together, the two women walked out of the kitchen, and began to mount the stairs.

Outside the study door, Owen Salusbury and Sir John Davies stood on guard, both looking worried.

'They are clamouring to be released—the Earl swore he'd be back within thirty minutes and here's a couple of hours gone by, and no sign of him,' Sir John told Penelope in a low voice. 'Certainly you may go in and speak to them, I hope you can make their imprisonment seem less tedious.'

Inside the study, the men were sitting round the table, playing cards. Egerton stood up and bowed, closely followed by Sir William Knollys, Lord Chief Justice Popham, and the Earl of Worcester.

The two women knew all four men well for they were all friends of Essex, often in and out of his house, and William Knollys was Lettice's brother and therefore Essex's uncle.

'Are you comfortable, gentlemen?' Penelope said with what brightness she could muster. 'I'm sorry my brother has kept you waiting, but be sure his delay is not of his making.'

'Delay?' roared William Knollys. 'Delay, you call it? We are hostages, niece! That young scamp of a brother of yours must be out of his mind. We came under the seal of England with a message from her Grace, and he has the infernal gall to lock us up as if we were common felons!'

'I know it seems very bad,' Penelope acknowledged. 'But when he has seen the Queen and explained to her himself, you will understand the need for this ... this temporary loss of liberty. I will have some wine brought up, and some bread and meat.'

'And have some logs brought, the fire is burning low and it's a cold day,' said the Earl of Worcester in his precise, finicking voice. 'I never thought to find Essex's hospitality sink so low, upon my word I did not!'

'Is your mother here?' demanded Sir William. 'And I should hope not, indeed!

At least I am not to be shamed by my own sister consenting to my imprisonment.'

Penelope thought she now understood more fully her mother's apparent defection.

'But why are *you* here, ladies?' the Lord Keeper said. 'If there is any trouble, and I fail to see how you are to avoid it, locking up the Queen's councillors, then this is the last place for any of you.'

'He is my brother,' and 'He is my husband,' both women replied in the same breath.

Egerton nodded slowly. 'Aye. But this is no place for women.'

Sir William looked sharply at Frances. 'Fanny here? Eh? I know that young fool Rutland is in it up to his neck. Follow my nephew like a lamb to slaughter that one would.'

'Yes, she's here,' Frances said quietly.

'Then get her *out*, Frances,' Sir William said forcefully. 'D'you understand?'

'Yes, and I'll take your advice. I can

make up some excuse to send her to Walsingham House I'm sure.'

The atmosphere in the little room imperceptibly relaxed. Frances slipped out of the door and the men turned back to their game of cards.

'And what about that wine, niece?' old Sir William said jovially. 'Fetch it up!'

★ ★ ★ ★

At dusk, Essex returned to the house. Penelope and Frances had just seen the hostages off in the care of Sir Ferdinand Gorges, who had scarcely bothered to greet them before rushing into the study, assuring Sir John Davies and the faithful Owen that he came with Essex's blessing to take the hostages back to speak for them to the Council.

So when Essex came up the garden, it did not occur to Penelope to mention the hostages. Instead, she said, 'Why, whatever has happened?'

267

For the little party presented a sorry sight. Essex himself was streaked with sweat and dirt, his garments loosened at the neck, his legs mired up to the knee. Mounteagle looked like a drowned rat, for in his hurry to get into the boats which they had managed to find moored by the Thames he had fallen into the river and very nearly drowned. Old Lord Sandys, pale and sick, had caught a chill and was shivering violently, and Southampton had been forced to jump into the water to pull the panicking Mounteagle out, so he, too, was drenched.

Penelope, clucking like a hen with one chick, hustled them into the small parlour where she and Frances had been sitting. In front of the fire, steaming and shivering, the men asked after the hostages, and were told by the dismayed women how they had been ushered out by Gorges minutes before Essex and his friends had returned.

Southampton began to rage, but Essex

said wearily, 'No matter, no matter. It is one blow amongst many to discover Gorges unfaithful. Well, we must barricade the house.'

'We already have, to the best of our ability,' Penelope said with simple pride. 'The house is surrounded, and there has been some shooting. But the courtyard holds them off. There are soldiers—our soldiers—defending the gates and walls.'

Even as she spoke there was a roar from outside. With one accord the men pushed and jostled out of the room, to rush across to the big dining hall which gave a view of the courtyard.

The Queen's men had broken down the gates and were entering the courtyard. Two men lay, bleeding, on the paving and even as Penelope drew in her breath with dismay a shot was fired which shattered the glass in the window and ricocheted round the room, causing Frances and Penelope to scream fervently.

'Get back, you girls,' Essex shouted.

'Thank God no-one was hurt! You must not approach the windows, do you hear? Bring some men in here, Sir John, and barricade the lower half of the windows at least. We will return to my study.'

Penelope, turning to obey, gave a gasp. On the floor lay Owen Salusbury. His face was turned away from her, but she had known him all her life, and would have recognised his dark, narrow head anywhere.

'Owen is hurt, Essex,' she said, dropping on her knees beside the wounded man. He turned his head at the sound of her voice, and her heart leapt. One side of his face had been ploughed by the bullet so that the cheekbone and skull were laid bare, and blood was pouring like scarlet water from a tap.

'Carry him upstairs,' she said to the men. 'Take him to a back bedroom, and Frances and I will do our best for him.'

For the next hour, she and Frances

stayed with the dying man, unable to relieve his pain, sick at heart to think that his gaiety and braveness had come to this, so that he lay like a dying animal, every breath a groan.

Across the bed Penelope met Frances's patient eyes, and for the first time for many years she thought of Philip Sidney, dying far from home, and thought that she had not been the only one to suffer; Frances had loved him too, and had shared his agony during those three terrible weeks.

'He is dead,' Frances said, bringing her thoughts back with a jerk to the present, and to the shell of Captain Owen Salusbury, at peace now, lying between them.

There had been more desultory firing, and a footman had been killed outright. There had been parleying, and the suggestion had been made that there should be a truce, for the women to be evacuated.

Now they walked downstairs and found

a line of maidservants, some giggling, some scared, waiting for the front door to be cleared of the barricades which had been piled up against it.

'I wish I'd had time to do my hair and tidy my gown,' Penelope said with an attempt at nonchalance. 'But there, I shall have to be imprisoned just as I am.'

'Bloody, but unbowed,' Southampton said cynically. 'You've got Salusbury's blood on your skirt, Penny, but you won't care for that. You're a seasoned warrior now.'

★ ★ ★ ★

By ten o'clock that same night it was all over; the maddening excitement, the heat of belief in a great cause, the deathly fear of 'them', the men who had been friends last week and would be friends next, but for twenty-four hours had been 'the enemy'.

Safely ensconced in Walsingham House, tired to death, they heard from one of the servants who had been amongst the last to leave the house what had happened.

'The Lords declared they would rather die than submit,' the man said. 'But they agreed to yield if they were promised a fair trial. The Earl of Essex went to his study and burned a lot of papers and documents whilst they were talking, and then they went out, one by one, and knelt before the Lord Admiral to hand over their swords. I think they were taken to Lambeth Palace; they went quietly away, on horseback I believe. It is over.'

He looked so woebegone that Penelope patted his shoulder, reflecting that he was no older than her own Lally—maybe even younger.

'Yes, it's over, Pikeworth,' she said gently. 'Now you may go to your bed in peace. You did your best for the Earl, as we all did, and now all we can do is pray for a fair trial.'

'I think I did my best,' the young man said falteringly. As he reached the doorway he turned and said something in a voice so low that Penelope could not catch the words.

'What was that, Pikeworth?' she said, but the door had already closed.

'I didn't hear what he said,' Penelope said to Frances, who was nearer the door. 'Was it important?'

'No, not important.' Penelope saw that tears had risen to the other woman's eyes, making them look bigger and darker than ever. 'He said, "But Henry Tracy died for him".'

Penelope looked at her. 'Henry Tracy?'

'Essex's page. Penny, he was all of ten years' old.'

Just at that moment, the death of a little lad almost unknown to her seemed the most poignant and cruel thing Penelope could have heard.

She laid her golden head on her arms and wept as if her heart would break.

TWELVE

Once the siege had ended, events moved incredibly quickly. Penelope was put under house arrest until the trial was over and all the ringleaders, including Essex, were condemned to death. She herself was also condemned to the Queen's extreme disfavour, for her part in the rebellion and for that much regretted letter. But as yet, her punishment was not decided; until it was, she was sent down to the country home of Mr Henry Lakeford, there to remain until the Lord Admiral had satisfied himself that she was not dangerous.

Even in the Lakeford's rigidly disapproving household she heard of Essex's death. He died bravely, they said. She held her head high and kept her shoulders straight, and would not allow tears to fall before these people, though she shed rivers in the privacy of her room at night.

His confession made it harder to bear. When Meg Lakeford, who was inclined to be friendly when no other members of her family were near, told Penelope how the Earl had told the Council everything, laying the blame on all his dearest friends, even revealed the relationship between his favourite sister and Charles Mountjoy, Penelope could hardly speak for shock.

'But he burnt his papers, diaries, everything, to make his friends safe,' Penelope whispered at last. 'He was determined to save his friends by denying any complicity.' She seized Meg's arm, gripping so tightly that her fingers dug through the material, making the older woman wince. 'Was he racked?'

'Why no, Lady Rich,' Meg said, a look of alarm chasing across her placid face. 'The Queen would never have allowed it, and besides, there was no need. He told his confessor all, then repeated it to the Council, even having certain of the conspirators brought in so that he could accuse them to their faces.'

'Dear God,' Penelope said softly. 'Dear God, his mind must have broken under the strain.'

'It is said that he told the Council Mountjoy was as guilty of treason as he, for he would have brought the army over to fight the Queen, had there been time, and had he been in England he would have taken part in the rebellion.'

'I hope the Council were not fools enough to believe it,' Penelope said. 'I can do nothing, now, for my brother, but I would not have him injure others even by his death. My mother's husband died too, but he was steadfast to the end, I believe?'

'That's right,' Meg said. She patted Penelope's shoulder diffidently. 'And Essex died repentant.'

'Yes,' Penelope said, turning away. When she thought of her brother's head lying on the block, patiently waiting for the blow that would end his confused and ruined life, she could only think of little Robert, her baby brother, lying in his bed, one night when she had roamed the house with the most appalling toothache. So soundly he had slept, thumb in mouth, cheeks rosy, secure in his little bed, his nurse within call. She hoped he slept as peacefully now, in his humble grave within the Tower walls.

'They say no-one in London has a good word for Francis Bacon,' Meg said presently. 'He was glad enough of the Earl's patronage, and took rich gifts from him. And then to stand up at his trial and condemn him! My father says he told some terrible lies in that soft, persuasive voice of his—and needlessly, for the Council knew that the Earl would be condemned.'

'I can imagine,' Penelope said. 'He is a poisonous creature. What of Southampton and Rutland? Is there any more news of them?'

'They're in the Tower, but like to

come out as soon as they pay their ransoms,' Meg replied. 'The Queen bears a grudge against Southampton still for his clandestine marriage, and his ransom is so high that he cannot meet it. He's made many an enemy, has the young Earl.'

★ ★ ★ ★

'I have had word from the Lord Admiral, Lady Rich, that you are free to go. I am glad, for your sake. This has been an uncomfortable time for you.'

'You've been most kind,' Penelope said politely, and saw from old Mr Lakeford's expression that he really was beginning to regard her with more sympathy.

'Not at all. I am to accompany you home to Leighs, where the Queen gives you into your husband's guardianship. I plan to set out at dawn tomorrow. Will that suit you?'

'Certainly,' Penelope said.

★ ★ ★ ★

Leighs looked as it always had; the most beautiful home set in perfect surroundings. Riding up the drive, Penelope thought that the Queen must be smiling to herself over the form her revenge had taken.

Sent home in disgrace, to the guardianship of the husband she had not lived with for several years!

How will he receive me, she wondered. Will he welcome me with open arms as the mother of his children and his most efficient housekeeper? Or will he resent my intrusion into his life?

But it was not Rich who greeted her, drawing her into the lady chamber, sending Mr Lakeford back to his wife with a good hot dinner inside him, it was her daughters.

'Robbie has gone with father to the cottages at Pig corner, to see about some ewes which have dropped lambs nearby. Father suspects that some of the cottagers marked their own dead lambs with his mark, and took our live ones for their own.'

Lally broke in, her green eyes twinkling. 'It may be true, mother, and Robbie may have winked at it! You see, father keeps the poor lad grievously short of money, and Dick Figgett is his particular friend. *We* think Letty and I, that Dick has been selling the odd lamb for our Robbie, and giving him the proceeds. We could not *imagine* where our Robbie got the money from to take his village wench gifts, and to go cock-fighting with Dick. But when father missed the lambs, we fancied we knew.'

'A woman? Robbie has a woman? But good God, the boy's only fourteen!'

'No, mother, not a *woman*, a lass about the same age as himself. Do you remember Ida Figgett, Dick's aunt? That red-headed wanton, you used to call her. Well, she had twin daughters just after you bore Robbie, she called them Mary and Molly, but Mary died when she was three. Our Robbie has been chasing after little Moll these six months, and now he says they've come to an understanding! All it really means, we think, is that they are excellent friends.'

'I hope so,' said Penelope. She had always harboured doubts about Ida Figgett's relationship with Rich, and now it occurred to her that Robbie might well find himself courting his half-sister. But Letty and Lally soon put her fears at rest.

'If you think that our father is also Molly's, you may rest easy,' Letty said frankly. 'But she is the spitting image of that Spanish-looking farmer who used to live up by the church. They say round here that he would have married Ida, but that he was killed by a bull before the twins were born.'

'And if the twins had been fathered by Rich,' Lally said with directness, 'They could scarcely have been dark-skinned and dark-haired, for he is fair and Ida is a red-head. Don't *worry*, mother!'

So when at last Penelope went to her old room, it was with a certain sense of pleasure that at least she would have the company of her beloved children whilst the Queen's displeasure lasted. She knew her Blount family were being well-looked after at Chartley, and that Lettice would not allow them to feel neglected.

So she bade a maid unpack a few of her things, telling her that Lavender would be arriving with a cartload of clothing within the next few days.

* * * *

When night-time came, Penelope was glad to be able to climb into her bed. Rich had returned from his visit to the cottage and had welcomed her politely enough. He had watched her playing with the younger children, Isabel and Essex, who were so alike it was almost comical. They both had long, fair hair, hazel eyes, and pointy, freckled faces, with expressions like mischievous mice. The little boys, Henry and Charles, competed for her hugs, wanting to be cuddled onto her lap, insisting in every game that they should sit one each side of mother.

They can scarcely remember the time when I lived here, and did not merely visit, Penelope thought remorsefully. Yet they are prepared to give me so much love! Henry, a stout, red-headed seven year old, was very much Rich's son in looks. Odd how attractive a square, unimaginative face can be on a child, when it suits his father so ill, she thought.

Charles, the baby, was different again; thin, dark, dreamy! Sometimes, Penelope thought, I wonder about Charles. *Could* I have made a mistake? *Could* Charles really be a Blount? But Rich had accepted him, and if he had a favourite, it was the youngest son who stood at his knee, arguing solemnly against going to bed now, 'because our muvver is here!'

Lavender had not arrived, so one of

the housemaids moved around the room, hanging up clothes, tidying away the water Penelope had used for washing, standing her hair-brushes side by side on the dressing-table.

Penelope bade her build up the fire, for it was a windy night, and snuff the branch of candles, leaving only the one beside the bed. Then she dismissed the girl and settled down to read over a book of household accounts before snuffing the candle.

She was involved in the complexity of the milk yield figures, when the door opened. She raised her eyes from the page, expecting to see Letty, or Lally, or perhaps both, but it was Rich.

'We've got to talk,' he said without preamble. 'I'll fetch a chair.'

He pulled one over beside the bed, and sat down.

She smiled at him encouragingly, but he did not at once begin, and it occurred to her that he was drunk. His smile was set, a little foolish, and his cheeks were very flushed.

'Well, Robert,' she said at last. 'What have we to talk about? It is a little late for a social call.'

'Are you here to stay, Penny, or just because the Queen has forced your hand?'

She did not pretend to misunderstand him.

'I am not returning to your bed, my dear. But I imagine that I shall be here for a protracted stay and so I will take over the management of the house and of your books once more, and entertain for you, so that the girls can begin to meet eligible young men. Is that in order?'

She could see he was taken aback by her frankness. He stared at her owlishly for a moment.

'Still fond of you,' he ventured at last. 'Still miss you like the very devil.'

'Well, I'm fond of you, in a way,' Penelope said with more tact than truthfulness. 'But you fill my place in your bed the moment I leave the house, Robert, you know you do! And I miss Leighs! So let us just say that I am home for a stay, at the Queen's pleasure, you might call it. I will work for my keep, as I have always done in the past.'

'No.'

She did not understand him. 'No, Robert? You mean you don't want my help with the books, or the house?'

'You come here as my wife in every sense, or you take yourself elsewhere.'

She gaped at him, wondering at his sudden change of heart, for he had taken her previous visits philosophically enough.

'I thought hard about the whole business, Penny, when the messenger arrived to say you were being sent home, and that I was to see you got up to no more mischief. By God, woman, I had a narrow escape from being mixed up in your brother's ugly business, d'you know that? If I had not been so ill that I had a good excuse for drawing back I could easily have been one of those named. But I knew something was wrong with Essex! I spotted it years ago, if not, I might have been faced with paying a whacking great fine which I could not have raised without crippling myself, or ...' He drew his hand across his throat in a speaking gesture.

'I know, Robert, I know. But it's over now, and we may all thank God that we've escaped. Essex is dead, and though I think he took leave of his senses towards the last, I still love him, and miss him. But I am heartily glad he didn't embroil you in his unfortunate affairs.'

'Aye, Penny, but *still* you miss the point. You were in it up to your pretty little neck, weren't you? He used you as a messenger, I know that! I've never known who your fancy man was, have I? Did he die with Essex, eh? Or are you hanging on the sleeve of Southampton, or Rutland, and waiting for them to emerge from confinement and take up with you once more?'

'What does it matter whom I love, save that you aren't the man?' Penelope said with more sharpness than she intended. 'I'm tired, Robert. Come to the point!'

'God, Penny, you can be slow-witted when you like. Can't you *see?* I have no *need* to put up with your alley-cat morals any more! I have no need to turn a blind eye when you rush off to Town to sleep with God knows who! Before, I dared not say too much for your brother was a man of importance, who could have twisted the facts so that I seemed the guilty party! He would never have stood for me making his sister known as an adultress. But he's dead, Penny! Dead and gone, and now you've got to stand on your own feet. It can be of no possible advantage to me now to pretend you are still my wife, for your reputation has whistled down the wind. You are not an asset, woman, you're a liability.'

'Then why did you ask if I would stay here as your wife?'

He got up from his chair and took a couple of strides across the room, so that he was standing with his back to her.

'Because I still *want* you,' he said forcibly. 'God help me, I'll risk the Queen's wrath to have you in my bed again, and by my side for the rest of my life.'

'I can't do it,' Penelope said, her voice breaking. 'You must repudiate me, then, and I'll have to find someone else willing to take me in. When must I go?'

'Tomorrow.'

She thought of the children, of Charles's wistful dark eyes gazing at her as she rode away. Bereft.

She began to plead, reminding him of the useful things she could do, how easy it would be for both of them to keep up a pretence just for a few days, perhaps a week.

'When I say tomorrow, I *mean* to-morrow,' he shouted, suddenly angry. 'And if you argue with me, you may go tonight.

Get out of my house, you whore!'

As he spoke he crossed the room and stood beside the bed, then with an abrupt, jerky gesture he ripped back the covers. 'Get out!' he said.

She said harshly, 'Get out of my room!' and he hit her, hard, across the mouth. She fell back on the pillows, feeling warm salt blood trickle from a cut lip. He knelt on the bed and hit her again, his mouth working.

'My village women are less whores than you,' he said between his teeth. 'They pay me well for the little kindnesses I do them.' He swung his leg over her, so that he was kneeling across her thighs. 'You want a night's lodging?' he hissed. 'Very well, I'll take my fee now.'

She tried to push him away, tried to dodge his mouth as it came down on hers, and he jerked back for a moment, hitting her viciously again so that for a moment the candle seemed like a brilliant firework display.

'There is only one way to tame a trollop,' he said, his mouth against her neck. 'I should have beaten you black and blue the first time you strayed.'

He did not speak again, save to command her to lie still.

* * * *

'I hope you are glad to see me, mother, because I may be here for some time. Rich has repudiated me, and will have me in his house no longer. The Queen forbids me to go to London, and I dare not ask my friends for hospitality in case I make things difficult for them, with the Queen. If you turn me out, I can journey up to Alnwick and throw myself on Dotty's mercy, but God knows what her husband would say to *two* Devereux women under one roof! It seems he finds one more than he can handle!'

Lettice looked across the room at her daughter. She saw the bruises which stained one cheek, the cut lip, the beginnings of a black eye.

'Poor Penny, so Rich found you out at last,' she said lightly. 'Of course you may stay here. It will be good to have your company and if you are agreeable we might send for your children; there is plenty of room at Drayton Bassett for us all.'

THIRTEEN

Elizabeth was dead at last, and James I reigned in her stead. There had been no bloodshed, no unpleasantness of any sort; Elizabeth had given her consent to his succeeding, and when he had ridden into England he was greeted everywhere with the greatest joy.

As soon as she could, Penelope had hurried from Drayton Bassett to London.

The welcome at court was balm to her pride. King James had not forgotten his 'fair Ryalta' who had corresponded with him so faithfully for so many years, assuring him of the Devereux loyalty. So when he saw her at his new court, her face still as beautiful as the portrait she had sent him some years before, he had made it plain that Lady Rich was a great favourite.

He knew of her affair with Charles and was pleased to quiz her with it, though in the friendliest way. He counted Mountjoy, he said, as one of his best and most trusted servants.

Penelope thought him pleasant enough, though not at all handsome. He had a lean, suspicious face and his figure was not impressive; he was not tall, and he had thin, bandy legs. His broad Scots accent robbed many of his remarks of the wisdom they might have contained for her, because she was only able to understand him with difficulty.

But the unreserved welcome he had

given her was so pleasant, after years of Elizabeth's dislike and suspicion, that Penelope felt she was the most fortunate of women. And when the King suggested that she and Lady Southampton might like to ride to Berwick to meet his wife and children as they journeyed into England, only one rejoinder was possible.

Penelope stayed only long enough to attend her sister-in-law's third wedding, and then she rode off with Elizabeth Vernon beside her, to meet Queen Anne.

Now, they stood in the window of their cramped and crowded lodging, watching the passing of the crowds who were streaming towards the city gate through which Anne would ride, and chatted.

'I would *really* have preferred to stay in London, with Henry,' Elizabeth sighed. Southampton had been in the tower almost two years, so James's pardoning and subsequent release of the Earl had not come one moment too soon for her.

'If I thought that Charles was home I'd

go mad,' agreed Penelope. 'He might be, Elizabeth, think of that! He might at this very moment be sitting down to dine at Wanstead, wondering why I'm not there to meet him.'

'Why Wanstead?'

'Because he bought it from Frances before she married Clanricarde, that's why,' Penelope said. 'I suppose he will have a house in London, too, now that James is on the throne, and so *very* pleased with the way Charles has handled affairs in Ireland. The first person for God knows how long to bring the Irish to heel, coming home with the rebel Tyrone by his side, to sue for a pardon from the King!'

'What of Frances? I've not met Robert de Burgh. Do you like him?'

'He is quiet, and gentlemanly, and Frances is head-over-heels in love with her elderly admirer, which is good enough for me. He loves Frances's family and wants nothing better than to live with her and the children in the country, keep his estates, and give his pretty young wife the peace of mind she so urgently needs. There, quite a character sketch.'

'I'm glad Frances has a sensible husband at last,' Elizabeth said. 'She deserves a good man if anyone does.'

'I'm sure they'll be happy,' Penelope said. 'We'd better go down now, or we'll miss the Queen's entry into the town. I wonder if she is as handsome as her portraits?'

* * * *

She was not, but scarcely anyone noticed it for the light-hearted, ash-blonde Queen was still only twenty-eight and what with her charming foreign accent and her natural gaiety, few realised that she was no beauty.

She took to Penelope at once and insisted that ladies Rich and Southampton give up their hired lodgings and move into her suite. She chatted constantly and expected her friends to do the same and under the influence of her confidences, Penelope's own story was soon told. She talked of her children by Rich and those by Mountjoy and found the Queen not at all shocked. She played with Princess Elizabeth, a lively seven-year-old with her mother's yellow hair and a pair of wide blue eyes which missed very little.

The journey down to London was a protracted one, but how differently they travelled from the mean, rushed journey up to Berwick! Penelope and Elizabeth continued to share Anne's accommodation, and Anne had nothing but the best. Yet long before their destination was reached, Penelope had grown tired of the journey, for news had reached her that Charles was indeed back in England. He would await her at Wanstead.

★ ★ ★ ★

Charles saw her mounting the steps in

front of the house, not bothering with grace or dignity but attacking them at the double, as though she could not wait another second.

He had been in the stables but had heard her coach drive up, and had run round to the front of the house, as eager as she.

'Pen!'

At his voice she checked, then spun round and careered down the stone steps, petticoats flying, hair bouncing, arms stretched out to him. As he reached the bottom of the flight she simply jumped down into his arms so that suddenly he was holding her, feeling her heart pounding close to his own, knowing she sobbed with joy to see him again after so long. He bent his head and kissed her, feeling the remembered softness of her lips, smelling the familiar scent of her warm body mingling with the crushed violets which were pinned to her lace.

Then it was time to hold her at arm's length, appraising her familiar beauty. She looked not a day older, he told himself, than the day he had first held her in his arms and known that she was his. Her thick, shining hair, bleached by the sun to the shade of Devonshire cream, showed no trace of white, her skin was as smooth and unlined as a child's. She smiled up at him, enjoying his scrutiny, her eyes guileless with love, her red lips parted, showing her small white teeth and the tip of her tongue.

He gulped. How could he ever have played with the idea of marrying that daughter of Ormonde who had been offered him? It had been a political match of course, but three years is a long time. Three years of beating through the Irish countryside, burning and despoiling, seeing the poor wretched peasants reduced to eating earth, and worse. He pushed to the back of his mind the recollections of cannibalism which he had discovered flourishing in one backward little hamlet. And in those three years he had been the oppressor; he might take a woman, but there could be no affection between oppressor and oppressed.

So he had toyed with the idea of the Ormonde marriage; an easier way to make peace, surely? But his heart was not in it, and the Ormondes, realising, had allowed the subject to drop.

As though she read his thoughts, Penelope said softly, 'Three years is a long time, my lord, but I have been faithful. My husband has repudiated me and now I believe there will be a divorce. But remember, there has never been more than love and trust between *us*. No binding contract on either side; you are as free as you ever were.'

Laughing, he put his arm around her shoulders and guided her up the steps and into the hall.

'We will talk of the Ormonde business if you wish,' he said below his breath. 'For myself, there is little to say but that I would never wed any woman but you.

And now my love, we are newly met after an intolerable absence! Are we to waste the night in *talk?*'

He heard her swallow, and felt her shrink closer to him; he smiled. They would not waste the night in talk.

★ ★ ★ ★

Within weeks of his return, Mountjoy had been raised to the position of Duke of Devonshire and Penelope took on the rank of Countess of Essex, since Frances was now Countess of Clanricarde.

At first, their joy knew no bounds, for to be the close friend of the Queen, as Penelope was, and to be a Privy Councillor, a Duke, and the confidant of the King, as Charles was, seemed sweeter for the years that had gone before.

Penelope became a Lady of the Bed-chamber and was always at court. Men and women who had ignored her of late years, begged her to intercede with the

King for them. She found it easy to talk to him now, for she understood his broad Scots and also his broad sense of humour. She speedily realised that a ready wit, a quick retort, might gain the favour already denied some sober citizen. Naturally quick-witted, therefore, she throve.

Essex House was given to the Duke of Devonshire for a town house, and Penelope became his hostess as a matter of course. She brought her Rich daughters to town for the winter season, and then her eldest Rich son. Her children by Mountjoy could live with her openly, and she and Charles became regular guests at houses where they had never thought to be acknowledged.

'Happy, Pen?' Charles asked her one night when they had returned from a ball at Whitehall Palace. 'You are popular on the dance floor, I scarcely saw you still for a moment, and couldn't get near enough to you to ask for a dance myself.'

'Yes, I'm happy,' Penelope said slowly.

'But though I cannot regret the passing of Elizabeth's court ...'

'I know what you mean. You are the centre, my heart's darling, but of what? The King hunts, but does not care to rule. I attend Council meetings, but James rarely appears. Can you imagine Queen Elizabeth missing a Council meeting? Nothing could be less likely.'

'They are kind, and amusing company, but they do not have the *dignity* of a King and Queen, Charles! Not only do they allow drunkenness amongst their courtiers, but they get drunk themselves. And though I know James cannot *help* dribbling wine out of the sides of his mouth, I sometimes think he does it worse than he need.'

'And that pageant—where the Queen fell off the side of the stage and just lay there, giggling,' Charles contributed. 'I know, my darling! Perhaps if the truth is known we are two old dogs who cannot learn new tricks. But I know many who agree with you.'

'It would be most unwise to show the slightest disapproval,' Penelope said at once. 'And I hope no-one but you has ever noticed that I *cannot* always dismiss such matters as of little account. And how folk would jeer at us if they knew! The Duke of Devonshire and his adultress, daring to criticise their betters!'

'I think it would be a good idea if we stopped chasing the King and Queen and rusticated for a while, with the children,' Charles said. 'Will that help?'

Instead of answering, she slid her arms round his neck and kissed his smiling mouth.

'Best and most understanding of creatures!' she said.

* * * *

'Well Charles, you may say it is no business of mine, and that the boy is Rich's responsibility, but he is as much my son as Robert's, and if I do not interfere I can

305

see that clod so antagonising the Hattons that they will forbid the marriage. Robbie is very attracted, you know. I've not met the girl, but he thinks her beautiful. And she's a considerable heiress. Not that that would weigh me, I assure you, were it not for Robbie's feelings.'

They were in the main bedroom at Essex House; the room where once, long ago, Captain Owen Salusbury had died of his wounds. But Penelope no longer thought of the past, the present was too full of event and excitement.

Penelope was engaged in twisting her side-hair into ringlets, watching the skill of her own fingers with admiration in her mirror. Charles dropped the flower he had been removing from his doublet into the waste-basket, and put his arms over her shoulders so that his fingers could fondle hers. She pushed his hands away and he squeezed her, smiling at her through the mirror.

'You don't have to justify your actions

to me, love! I've not accused you of interfering, nor shall I! Of course, as Robbie's mother, you have a right to help him in any way you can. That is not interfering!'

'Well, I *shall* interfere,' Penelope said firmly. 'But do you mind, my dear love, if we spend Christmas at Whitehall, with the court? I know we'd planned to go to Wanstead until the New Year, but ...'

'It isn't politic to spend Christmas anywhere but court, unfortunately,' Charles said gloomily. 'There is to be a grand masque for twelfth night, and that means I shall have to see you cavorting on the stage with scarcely anything on, for all the men to ogle. I *think* Queen Anne wants you to be a dusky maiden, and she is certainly going to be black.'

Penelope groaned. 'Oh, no! I rather enjoy masques, with everyone staring and wondering how on earth I keep my figure, and you watching the men watching me. But I draw the line at black paint! It is sticky and hot, and the very devil to remove.'

'Why don't you draw the line at appearing in these masques altogether?' Charles said hopefully. 'But I know, you cannot do so without offending the Queen. Very well, but I warn you, when we are married it will be a different story. I shall not *allow* my wife to play a part and the Queen will just have to find someone else.'

'When we marry! *If* we marry, you mean. Why did you mention it?'

'Because there is now little doubt that Rich will get his divorce and thus you will get yours. God knows, he's trying hard enough! And if you do get a divorce, I cannot see *this* monarch objecting to our re-marriage! He has been delighted to have his Queen befriend you above all other English ladies, and he has welcomed your children, both legitimate and illegitimate, into his court. I am sure that he would welcome our tying the knot legally, at last.'

★ ★ ★ ★

Afterwards, both Fanny Hatton and Robbie agreed that it was entirely due to Lady Rich that their marriage took place. Beautifully dressed, gay and fun-loving, and the most understanding woman in the world, she entertained Fanny in her own home, took her to informal supper parties given by the best known and most respected of James's councillors, and introduced her to society. And Robbie, of course, was constantly by her side.

When she suggested to Queen Anne that the young couple might marry, Anne said with a sentimental sigh, 'Such a match would be delightful. Your Robbie is *very* good-looking, Lady Rich! But the girl's grandfather, Sir Francis Gaudy, is negotiating with Lord Treasurer Dorset, to match his grandson, Richard, with Mistress Hatton. But there, your son is a fine lad and will console himself soon enough.'

Penelope smiled sweetly, and told Anne, apparently apropos of something quite different, that she herself had been forced into a loveless match when not much older than Fanny.

'It might have ruined my life, had I not met Charles,' she said, and hoped that the Queen might never lay her hands on Philip's sonnets!

Her next move was to suggest a secret marriage to the young people, though not directly. She spoke to Fanny when they were driving back to Whitehall one evening after witnessing a play at the Globe theatre.

White moonlight flooded the carriage, and Penelope had made sure that Robbie rode his horse alongside them, so that he was not within earshot.

'Robbie's grandmother, Lady Leicester, made a secret marriage, and was *so* happy, despite royal displeasure,' she told the impressionable girl. She went on to describe the chapel at Wanstead where the knot had been tied, told Fanny of Dotty's mad elopement—only she made it sound as romantic as the moon above—and finished by grimly warning of the miseries of a loveless match.

To Robbie she was more practical, merely telling him that Dorset's grandson was in hot pursuit of the lovely Fanny, and with parental consent, too.

'So perhaps it would be better to look elsewhere,' she said with careful tactlessness, and knew half the battle won when Robbie glowered at her, muttering that Richard Dorset was a weedy youth, and not man enough to bed a marigold, let alone a pretty girl.

Within a week, Robbie approached her, asking for her assistance at a runaway marriage between himself and Fanny.

'I love her with all my heart, and she me,' he declared.

She had pretended horror, and a reluctance to assist, but it was she who arranged for a clergyman to perform the ceremony at Wanstead, and saw the young people depart from a supper party, knowing that her son was not escorting mistress Hatton to her home, but to an illicit marriage.

For a while after the marriage had been effected, the Hattons, Gaudys and the unfortunate Dorsets were very annoyed. To her surprise, Rich was equally furious with her, loudly proclaiming that it was none of *his* doing, Devonshire's mistress had planned the entire thing.

'Devonshire's mistress' knew that her husband felt slighted, and thought he had been made to appear of little account in the affairs of his son and heir, but she thought he had been well served.

'It is perfectly true that I took over the handling of my son's love affair,' she said to the Queen. 'But from whom? Your Majesty, Rich had done *nothing* for the boy; refused to enter into negotiations, did not attempt to befriend the girl or interest the parents in Robbie's prospects. After all, it is a good match for both, and a love match into the bargain.'

And she soon had the satisfaction of seeing both the King and Queen publicly greet the young couple and wish them every happiness, and to further please her, the King congratulated her on furthering such an excellent match.

'You will get above yourself, my pretty Pen,' Charles told her, squeezing her shoulders. 'Next thing I know, you will be refusing to paint yourself black for the next masque, but will tell the Queen you are an albino blackamoor!'

'In the next masque I am Aphrodite, rising from a sea of beech-green gauze,' Penelope said.

'And very little else, I suppose,' Charles said gloomily. 'You have the most beautiful breasts and I love to feast my eyes on them, but not when half the court is doing the same.'

'I shall wear a flesh coloured bodice,'

Penelope protested. 'Low cut, of course.'

'Will you dance?'

Laughingly, she flicked his nose with her finger. 'Don't *worry!* I'm not getting any younger. Soon enough no-one will suggest that I dance on the stage half-clothed with the Queen and her ladies, comparing my charms with those of women ten years younger than myself. Wrinkles and grey hair will put a stop to all that.'

But her tone lacked conviction and Charles, reaching for her hand, thought he had never known a woman lovelier.

★ ★ ★ ★

The messenger rode down the drive again, his task completed, and Penelope tore open the document he had brought her.

Seconds later she was running up the stairs and into Charles's study, her cheeks pink with excitement.

'Charles! The divorce has been granted. The Queen has written that she is delighted for me, and so is the King.'

Charles turned from his desk, smiling indulgently at her.

'And what difference does this make, Pen? I could not love you more.'

'Well, but Charles, I shall be a grandmother in a few weeks, when Fanny's child is born. Shall we ... shall we venture?'

'But do I *want* to marry a grandmother?' Charles said solemnly. 'And if we do decide to wed we shall do so quietly and without fuss. Your first husband would make trouble for us if he could.'

Penelope pouted. 'But if I am divorced, who can make trouble?'

'Practically anyone, I should think! This divorce does not mean you are free to re-marry, remember. Oh, I know Henry VIII did so, but he legalised murder in his own interests! But we have lived together as man and wife for so long, now, that I think marriage would merely legalise the connection.'

'Laud is your private chaplain, isn't he?

Well, we could marry quietly, at Wanstead. I love the little chapel there, where my mother married Leicester, and dear Elizabeth Vernon married Southampton. And Charles, the children could act as my attendants—the girls, at any rate.'

'Quiet weddings do not call for attendants; and it is not at all the thing to have one's children present at one's nuptials, let alone attending upon the bride! Sometimes I think you are as lost to propriety as ...'

'As the Queen?' interrupted Penelope, smiling up at him. 'She cares little for convention, and nor do I. Then we are to be married, Charles?'

Delighting in her pleasure, he nodded gravely. 'Aye, since you wish it. I will instruct secretary Morrison to look after my affairs whilst we are away. And my man shall pack for me whilst Lavender does likewise for you.'

'Shall I write and invite mother to be present?'

He was indulgent, amused that a ceremony could mean so much to her.

'If you wish, but the messenger must ride swiftly or Lady Leicester will be arriving in the middle of our honeymoon, and that would never do!'

She had been walking towards the door but now she turned and ran back to him, flinging her arms around his neck.

'Darling, *darling* Charles!' she said breathlessly.

★ ★ ★ ★

They lay together in their big bed at Wanstead, the bedcurtains pulled back so that they could see the bright stars shining in the night sky beyond their window.

'Charles, are you still awake?'

'Yes, my dear love. Are you happy?'

'Oh, *so* happy! Tell me, Charles, is it better with your wife than with your mistress?'

'Is it ... Oh, I see. I need notice of that question. I was a bachelor until this morning, you see.'

There was a short silence. She lay quiet, listening to her breathing, and the thud of his heart beat, so close that it seemed within her own breast.

'Charles?'

'Yes, love?'

'I wish I had been a maid, so that you could have been the first.'

He took her in his arms, kissing her brow, her ear, her neck.

'Foolish Pen! One love, that is what matters! I have had many women, you have known other men. But when the day of judgement comes, can you say that you had one perfect love, which transcended all the rest? I can.'

'Oh, Charles, and I! Compared with my feelings for you, the rest are dreams.'

'Then nothing else matters, love.'

★ ★ ★ ★

'It is worse that I had ever dreamed,' Penelope said hopelessly. She walked across Elizabeth's luxurious parlour at Southampton House, with the window which overlooked a busy stretch of the Thames, and pressed her nose to the glass, pretending interest in passing river traffic.

'What did they say? Have you had an audience with them since your marriage?'

'Anne smuggled me a note, and I met her secretly in her own chamber. She was very sweet really. She cried, and hugged me, and wished me happy, but said that I never should have done it. She said she'd lost her dearest friend, and that I must never come to court again, unless the situation altered. We must say goodbye, she said, until the King relents, in happier times.'

'Happier times? Does she mean by any chance after Rich's death? For surely, only that will make you a widow, able to marry

Charles without let or hindrance?'

Penelope smiled. 'I suppose so. But if only the King had chosen some other way of showing his disapproval! To treat me like an abandoned woman and Charles like a wretch in front of the whole court has humiliated us both. And I *cannot* understand the logic of it! He welcomed me at court, and allowed his wife to befriend me; he put me before the most important people in the land! And he teased me about living with Charles, he met my Blount children, he visited us at Essex House. Yet when we marry! It is *hard*, Elizabeth.'

'The King's vanity is hurt I believe, rather than his sense of propriety,' Elizabeth said reassuringly. 'If Charles had only consulted him before taking such a step! If the Solomon of Europe had said he would not countenance the union, then it could have been dispensed with, for you and Charles were so happy, Penny! Or you could have married and kept it a secret—who would have known? But now ...'

'Now we must just make the best of it,' Penelope interrupted. 'If it were not that we are under a cloud we could enjoy rustication, indeed we could! I had had enough of court life, with men pawing me, and the King more often drunk than not. And his endless progresses, always moving on to some new hunting spot, with few amenities and fewer modern conveniences! And that hunting! James either risking his neck on horseback chasing after the hounds and then behaving in a disgusting way when they killed, or being too worn out to get up from his bed so that he lolled there all day, with one of his young boys dancing attendance on him!'

'What *did* he do when they killed?' asked Elizabeth, glad to give Penelope's thoughts a more cheerful turn. 'I'm not often at court, and not fond of blood-sports, so I've never accompanied a royal hunt.'

'Oh, he throws himself at the stag as though it had injured him personally, cuts its throat and puts his hands in the stream of the life-blood. Then he slits open its belly and paddles in the stomach contents and entrails,' Penelope said, wrinkling her nose. 'Imagine it, Elizabeth! And he very rarely washes. I can tell you I shan't be sorry if I never see a royal hunt again!'

'You are best out of it,' Elizabeth agreed. 'And what of his favourites, Penny? I've heard he pays women extravagant compliments, and is extraordinarily interested in all facets of one's private life, but the talk goes that his real interest is in men!'

'He is curious about women,' Penelope said. 'But it is men he kisses and fondles, believe me! Young lads, some of them, whose mothers would writhe to see them behave so. But there, the Queen doesn't complain, or not now, at any rate, though I believe she used to break her heart at first. Now, I expect she prefers his absence to his presence—I know I would!'

The two women settled down to enjoy a gossip, and Elizabeth was relieved to see her cousin was looking happier.

She had come to Wanstead because she loved Penelope and wished to show the world that their disgrace would not alienate their true friends, but also because Charles had sent her a note.

'Cheer Pen up if you can,' he had written. 'She feels the disgrace doubly because she blames herself for it. What rubbish, when my greatest desire has ever been to call her my wife! The King is merely piqued, and will come round before long, but meanwhile, comfort her for me.'

Charles was at Essex House, dealing with business matters, but the King had told him that Penelope should never again be installed there; so he worked on alone, forbidden to go to court, worrying that his wife might be reproaching herself every moment for his situation.

But already, one thing was clear to Elizabeth. Penelope's unhappiness was due only to the fact that their disgrace had made Charles's life more difficult. Nothing could mar her joy in her marriage, or the pleasure she got in being settled at last, with her children and the man she adored, at Wanstead.

★ ★ ★ ★

Time passed, in growing contentment. Friends began to call again at Wanstead, the children, knowing nothing of the King's displeasure, needed teaching, amusing, and occasionally, disciplining. Penelope's Rich offspring came to call. Letty brought her husband and stayed for weeks, Lally came with her betrothed. The young heir and his wife brought their child to see his grandmother, and told her, proud but shy, that another child was on the way.

324

Affairs of the court became no more than rumours. The gunpowder plot was tutted over, and the plot to capture the Princess Elizabeth and put her on the throne instead of her father was less than a nine days wonder, because Penelope's favourite mare dropped a foal on the fifth of November, and it was sickly and needed all their attention for weeks.

Then Charles returned from one of his periodical visits to London with a severe attack of bronchitis. Chest wheezing, voice all but gone, he was tucked up in bed by an anxious Penelope, and nursed with the utmost devotion.

She knew he was very ill, but he was strong, and his constitution had overcome worse attacks. She thought his chance of recovery excellent, but nevertheless she moved into a truckle bed beside their own comfortable fourposter, so that he might have plenty of room to move about, yet she was still near him.

Propped up in bed to ease his breathing,

he seemed to be gaining strength satis-factorily. Then, one night, Penelope was sitting before the fire dozing over some mending, when she heard a faint call from the bed. She hurried to his side, and raised him on his pillows.

'Pen?' he asked feebly. 'Always loved you, Pen. Never doubted you. You shall have it all, all!'

'I only want you,' Penelope said softly, smoothing his hot brow. 'You must fight, my love, and send this illness to the devil, where it belongs.'

He gasped, thickly, and shook his head. She heard the bubbling of his chest each time he drew breath.

'Cannot ... fight ... harder,' he muttered. 'Where ... Mountjoy?'

'Asleep in bed, where he should be,' Penelope said. 'I will call the maidservant to fetch the doctor.'

'Yes,' he murmured. 'But don't ... leave me, Pen.'

She ran quickly to the door, called and

ran back to the bedside, her face showing anxiety, though she strove to hide it.

'I'm a ... lucky fellow,' he said huskily. 'Lucky.'

His eyes moved sideways and Penelope followed his glance. On the opposite side of the bed, she thought she saw a woman standing, dressed in black, with a sweet, heart-shaped face, but when she looked harder, there was nothing there. Only the dark blue bedcurtains, moving slightly in the draught from the still open door.

'Take ... care ... of ...' the words seemed to be dragged from him, and she hung over the bed, gazing anxiously into his shadowed eyes.

'Take care of the children? Of course I will, my sweet love.'

He tried to shake his head, then drew in another rasping, ragged breath.

'Take ... care ... of ... yourself,' he said with agonised triumph. Then his lids shuttered the black eyes she loved so well, and she knew he was dead.

FOURTEEN

Summer and autumn are meeting at last, Penelope thought, as she strolled through the Wanstead gardens and into the orchard. Overhead, the rich harvest of apples hung, soon to be picked and stored in straw, another task for her to deal with.

She had been busy, these past five months, but at last she was beginning to feel that the estate was taking shape and would run without Charles.

Remembering how she had dragged herself back to life after his death was painful, as the surge of life is to a limb which has had its bloodflow cut off; but she had returned from the world of darkness which she had entered when he left her. She could remember little save that she had barely realised his death before the doctor had entered the room, too late to save Charles but in time to save her.

They told her that she had curled up in a corner of the room and refused food for two days, weeping and moaning. The children, terrified, had been kept from her until someone had the brainwave of sending Mountjoy into the room.

She remembered that; the small, pale-faced boy pulling insistently at her hand, telling her that she must come; her youngest son, St John had swallowed a feather, and was choking.

It had been true, though he had not mentioned that her mother was there, dealing with the emergency by hanging St John upside down and hitting him sharply on the back.

She had clasped the little boy close, until his frightened squalls had turned to hiccups. Then she had gone upstairs, not to the room she had shared with Charles but to her mother's chamber. She had called for Lavender and together they had repaired the ravages caused by two days of total neglect.

She returned to her place as head of the household, after that. Working as Charles would have wished, towards the smooth running of the estate.

She had not attended the huge state funeral which had been held in London, nor had she visited his grave in St Paul's chapel, Westminster Abbey. She had no desire to return to court, despite the Queen's intimation that she might do so.

Instead, she wrote to Cecil, asking his advice about replacing a thieving bailiff, and the man he had recommended was already proving his worth. She had brought Mountjoy to the King's attention, however, in a letter, and he had written back, a friendly enough note, saying that the lad should not be forgotten. Within weeks the boy had been created Lord Mountjoy of Mountjoy Fort, in Ireland. Charles had left the children well provided for, and she herself had Wanstead, and everything else which he was able to leave her.

And now? she thought. What does life hold for me, now? She had told her mother about the woman's figure which she had seen on the far side of Charles's bed the night he died, and Lettice told her again, as she had been told before, that some Devereux women had always had the power of foretelling their own deaths.

'They see themselves,' she said. '*Was* it like a reflection, Penny?'

'It is hard to tell, so misty was she,' Penelope said slowly. 'But she wore black, mother, and that day I was wearing blue.'

'You've worn black ever since Charles's death, though,' her mother reminded her.

'The point is, mother, that I did not die,' Penelope said, with such wistfulness in her tone that Lettice's heart bled for her.

'No, but a part of you did,' she said gently.

'Oh yes, a part of me is dead, and will never wake again,' Penelope said.

So now, she went on walking through

the orchard, though the pale green of twilight was filling the sky and the sun had long since gone down into a bed of fire.

The beauty of the sky was such that it drained the landscape of interest, and she walked on, watching the colours being sucked from the heavens, almost mesmerised by the beauty of it; into the birch pasture, where the young birch trees stood black against the sky, their first leaves already gilded and dropping.

At last, she turned back towards the house. She felt expectant, as though she waited for something, or someone.

And just ahead of her she saw a woman, dressed in black. She seemed very like the figure which had appeared beside Charles's bed, that night. Unafraid, filled only with dreamlike interest, Penelope went towards the other. For a moment they were face to face, and Penelope saw a woman with a pale face of great beauty, and pale hair, robbed of colour by the deepening twilight.

She smiled, and it was like smiling into a mirror, for the other smiled back.

They stood for a moment, facing each other, and then a voice called from the house and the spell was broken.

Penelope turned to look towards her home and when she looked back, she was alone.

Or was she alone? She seemed to feel a kindly, reassuring presence walking close beside her, as she returned to the house.

Her question had been answered; she had asked what life still held for her, and the answer was, death. Once, it would have frightened her; now she went to death willingly, because she knew her half-life was nothing to lose, and whatever price she might have to pay for her life as she had lived it, at the end of it all, there would be Charles.

The publishers hope that this book has given you enjoyable reading. Large Print Books are especially designed to be as easy to see and hold as possible. If you wish a complete list of our books, please ask at your local library or write directly to: Dales Large Print Books, Long Preston, North Yorkshire, BD23 4ND, England.

This Large Print Book for the Partially sighted, who cannot read normal print, is published under the auspices of

THE ULVERSCROFT FOUNDATION